CW00819794

POISONED

BY THE

BOOK

POISONED BY THE BOOK

NORTH DAKOTA LIBRARY MYSTERIES
NUMBER 2

ELLEN JACOBSON

Poisoned by the Book
Copyright © 2024 by Ellen Jacobson

All rights reserved. This book or any portion thereof may not
be reproduced or used in any manner whatsoever without the
express written permission of the publisher except for the use
of brief quotations in a book review.

This book is a work of fiction. Names, characters, places, and
incidents either are products of the author's imagination or
are used fictitiously. Any resemblance to actual persons,
living or dead, events, or locales is entirely coincidental.

Digital ISBN: 978-1-951495-53-4
Print ISBN: 978-1-951495-56-5
Large Print ISBN: 978-1-951495-57-2

Editor: Alecia Goodman, UnderWraps Publishing Services

Cover: Molly Burton, Cozy Cover Designs

Published by: Ellen Jacobson
www.ellenjacobsonauthor.com

For everyone who loves the smell of old books.

CONTENTS

CHAPTER 1
PAPER CUTS ARE THE WORST

"Medic! I need a medic, here!" Ray Koch yelled, his normally deep voice shrill. The middle-aged man collapsed onto the carpeted floor, holding his right hand above his head. "The pain. It's excruciating."

"Thea, call nine-one-one," my grandmother ordered as she rushed over to help Ray. Kneeling down next to the beefy man, Grandma gently laid a hand on his shoulder. "Where does it hurt? Is it your chest? Are you having a heart attack?" She spoke in soft and calm tones, reflecting her years of experience as a librarian in our small North Dakotan town before her retirement.

While I communicated with emergency services, I looked around the cramped room. Although it was the larger of the two library meeting rooms, it was jam-packed with boxes of used books—making it feel small and confining. With the annual book sale less than two weeks away, donations were coming in fast and furious. How were the EMTs going to fit in here with their equipment and stretcher?

"It's not my heart, Rose. A heart attack would be a walk in the park compared to this," Ray moaned as he thrust his fleshy hand in my grandmother's direction.

After inspecting his finger, Grandma said dryly, "It's only a paper cut, dear. Come on, get up. We'll go find the first aid kit."

Ray looked dubious. "Are you sure that's all it is, darlin'?" His Texan accent seemed more pronounced than normal. Perhaps it was due to all the pain caused by the tiny cut on his finger.

"Yes, dear. I know a paper cut when I see one. Occupational hazard." When Ray groaned as he got to his feet, she joked, "Don't you think you're being a little dramatic? Maybe instead of being president of the Garden Club, you should audition for the musical the theater group is putting on."

Ray gave her a faint smile as Grandma looped her arm through his. She turned to look at me, and I said, "Already on it. Calling nine-one-one back."

After explaining to emergency services they were no longer needed, I took a deep breath. Ray was such a hypochondriac. Odds were he wouldn't be back to help with the book sale prep tonight, maybe not even the rest of the weekend. He'd probably milk his recovery from the paper cut for all it was worth too.

The library was already struggling to get enough volunteers for regular duties. Finding folks who wanted to work special events, such as the book sale, was proving near impossible. My grandmother had twisted Ray's arm into spending his Friday night helping by tantalizing him with the promise of pizza and her famous rhubarb cookies once we had finished.

Now with Ray out of the picture, would we be able to get everything ready in time for the book sale? It was one of the main fundraisers of the year. With the recent budget cuts and fewer financial donations, the library was counting on it being a success.

A high-pitched, squeaky woman's voice behind me interrupted my train of thought. "Here's another one for you, Thea."

I turned and smiled wearily as Cassidy Dahl set a cardboard box on one of the folding tables lining the walls. The table groaned under the weight, but luckily didn't collapse. I glanced at broken laminate and metal pieces piled in the corner, proof there was a limit to how many boxes of books a table could hold.

"Thanks, I think." I studied the other woman. The soft-spoken, lanky brunette was in her early twenties. The default expression on her flawlessly made-up face was one of utter boredom. Books held zero interest for her. Why she was volunteering at the library was a total mystery, but I was glad she was here.

"We really appreciate your help, especially on a

Friday night." As I grabbed a box cutter, I mentally cringed at my use of 'we.' It's not like I was in charge of the place. Although, considering my family had founded the library in the late 1800s, I felt some sense of ownership.

Cassidy shrugged. "It's not like there's much else to do here on the weekends. I can't wait until I save up enough to move to Minneapolis and go to cosmetology school."

I couldn't argue with her. Our small town of Why wasn't exactly known for its nightlife. Sure, you could go bowling or to the movies, grab a pizza or burgers at one of the local joints, or take a drive to look at the wind turbines and oil derricks scattered in the fields around this part of western North Dakota. You could visit Bismarck or Fargo—they had more to offer. But if you wanted to eat at a fancy restaurant, do some serious shopping, see the Minnesota Twins play in person, hear live music, or check out nationally renowned cultural attractions, you needed to cross the state line. Minneapolis was where it was at. I should know, having lived there for several years before I moved back home.

On the other hand, life in Why had its positives. There were the usual things you find in small towns–a slower pace of life and a tight-knit community who looked out for each other. But we also had some unique attractions such as the taxidermy museum, my grandfather's giant ball of twine, our annual

Scandinavian festival, and a needy buffalo who wandered freely around town looking for handouts.

"I assumed a cute girl like you would have a date." As soon as the words escaped my mouth, I grimaced. Could I sound any more ridiculous? Asking Cassidy why she wasn't out with some guy made me sound like I was her mother. Not that I was old enough to have given birth to her. I was about seven, maybe eight years her senior. "Sorry. That made me sound so ... um ..."

"Old?" Cassidy suggested.

"Well, I was going to go with prying, but old sounds better. I think." I held up my hands. "Your love life is your business."

"Don't worry. If I had one, I'd tell you all about it. But I don't." Cassidy grinned. "What about you? Why aren't you out on a hot date?"

My cheeks grew warm as my thoughts drifted to Hudson Carter, the new library director and recent transplant from Florida. He certainly fell into the hot category with his unruly dark curly hair, an extensive collection of cardigans, and a vast knowledge of literature.

Okay, I realize that makes Hudson sound more nerdy than hot, but nerdiness can be hot, don't you think? Is there anything sexier than a guy reading a book? Not that I'm aware of.

When Hudson moved to Why during the winter to take up the library director role after my grandmother retired, we had become friends. Good friends. The kind of friendship you only develop when you solve a murder together. But we would never be more than friends. The man was a widower, after all. After losing your wife and unborn child, are you ever ready to date again?

"Earth to Thea," Cassidy said. "Thinking about someone in particular?"

"Of course not," I said a little too quickly, using the box cutter to slice the packing tape open on a box. "Just wondering what's inside here."

Cassidy tucked her long hair behind her ears. "I bet it's another set of dusty encyclopedias. It's hard to believe that's how people used to look stuff up back in the old days. Thank goodness we have our cell phones nowadays."

I chuckled. "Don't let my grandmother hear you say that. She's rather fond of encyclopedias."

"Well, sure. She's a librarian," Cassidy said. "They're old-fashioned that way."

Someone cleared their throat behind us. "Who are you calling old-fashioned?"

I spun around and saw my grandmother. She folded her arms across her chest, trying to repress a smile while giving Cassidy a stern look. Grandma looked neat and put together, as usual. Her light purple skirt, mint green blouse, and floral-patterned scarf hinted at the spring weather we all hoped was on its way to stay.

Cassidy's cheeks reddened. "Oh, I'm so sorry, Mrs. Olson. I didn't mean, um ... for you to, um—"

"Just because I was born long before you doesn't mean I'm old-fashioned," my grandmother said, cutting Cassidy off. Then she furrowed her brow. "But maybe you can explain what a cell phone is to me. I've never heard of those. Sounds awfully strange. Is it made out of actual cells? Do they grow them in petri dishes?"

"Phones made out of living tissue?" The expression on Cassidy's face conveyed a mix of utter confusion and shock. She pulled her own phone out of the pocket of her jeans and handed it to my grandmother. "No, they're made out of plastic and metal."

Grandma stared at Cassidy's phone as though she had never seen such a contraption before. "How strange."

Cassidy shot me a pleading look, and I put her out of her misery. "My grandmother is messing with you. She knows perfectly well what a cell phone is. You should see all the apps she has on hers. Scrabble and Wordle are her favorites."

"Don't forget my crossword puzzle app," Grandma added and turned to Cassidy. "I'm sorry for teasing you. People always think librarians are stuck in the past. That's not actually the case. We use technology just like the rest of the world. Of course, between you and me, I still think physical books are better than ebooks by a country mile."

My grandmother handed Cassidy back her phone, and adjusted the silk scarf knotted around her neck. "Although I shouldn't say 'we.' I'm not a librarian anymore," she said glumly.

"Grandma, just because you're retired doesn't mean you're not still a librarian," I said.

"Thea is right," a man agreed. I turned and saw Hudson in the doorway, adjusting the cartons stacked on his dolly. "Aren't you the one who always says that librarians are the guardians of a community's heart and soul? I've never met anyone who fits that description better than you. Being retired is simply your employment status. It's not who you are."

My grandmother beamed at Hudson as he pushed the dolly into the room. "You're sweet."

"That's only because you feed me so many of your home-baked cookies. All that sugar is bound to make anyone sweet." Hudson parked the hand cart next to one of the tables, then rubbed his stomach. "I'm starting to develop a paunch, though. Maybe middle age is setting in."

"Middle age?" I scoffed. "Get out of here. You're only a few years older than me, and there's no way I'm middle-aged."

"You might feel differently once you turn thirty," Hudson said.

Ignoring Hudson's comment about my upcoming birthday, I turned to my grandmother. "How's Ray?"

"He's fine. I got him a bandage, then brewed him

some coffee. He's sitting in the staff kitchen recuperating."

Hudson furrowed his brow. "What happened?"

"A paper cut. Nothing to worry about." Grandma rolled her eyes. "Although Ray did say he wasn't sure if he'd be back this weekend. He needs to rest up his finger for gardening season."

"I guess it's just you and me," I said to Cassidy.

"Uh-huh," Cassidy said without looking up from her phone.

"I'll make some calls and see if I can convince anyone else to help out." Grandma inspected the boxes on the dolly. "Where did these come from?"

"Martha Lund donated them," Hudson said. "She also said there's more where these came from."

As Hudson began lifting the boxes onto one of the tables, my grandmother and I exchanged glances. Martha willingly giving up her books? Not likely.

"Are you sure it was Martha who donated these books?" Grandma asked him.

"Yeah. She emailed me yesterday about it," Hudson said. "She said she'll bring more by next week. This was all she could fit in the trunk of her car, so it will take a few trips."

"Martha drove here?" My grandmother shook her head. "No, that can't be."

"What did this woman look like?" I asked.

"I'm not good at describing people." Hudson scratched his head. "I don't know. She's probably in her late thirties or early forties. Her hair is a dark auburn, and she wears it in loose curls. Let's see, what else? She has really striking eyes. They're green. Oh, and I loved her accent. Sounded like she's originally from somewhere in the Caribbean."

Grandma stared at Hudson. "That woman was *not* Martha Lund. Martha doesn't drive anymore. She's in her late eighties, of Norwegian descent, has silver hair, and the only striking thing about her eyes is the fact that she has cataracts."

"Oh, I had assumed the woman in the car was Martha, but she was in a rush, so we only had a brief conversation," Hudson said. "Maybe Martha had someone drop the boxes off for her?"

My grandmother pondered this. "Perhaps it was her new live-in nurse."

"What happened to the last one?" I asked.

"The word around town is that Martha fired her after she borrowed one of Martha's books without asking." Grandma leaned forward and said in a conspiratorial tone, "But that wasn't the worst of it. The gal had the audacity to dog-ear the pages."

"Seriously? She fired someone over folding a piece of paper?" Cassidy scoffed.

My grandmother put her hand to her chest and gasped.

"Dog-earing pages is sacrilegious to serious book lovers," Hudson explained to Cassidy.

"There's a reason why bookmarks were invented,"

Grandma stated primly. "You can grab a free one at the front desk."

"You don't have that problem when you read books on your phone," Cassidy said. "No paper cuts, either."

Before my grandmother could get on her soapbox about why physical books were superior to electronic ones, I interrupted. "Getting back to the lady who dropped off the books, it still doesn't make any sense."

"What do you mean?" Hudson asked.

"Martha is what you would call a hoarder when it comes to books," I said.

"I prefer to think of her as a collector," Grandma interjected.

"Okay, Martha is an avid *collector*," I said. "But not the kind of collector who sells any of her books, let alone donates them. In fact, every year she comes to the book sale and buys new ones to add to her shelves."

"This is completely out of character for Martha." My grandmother frowned. "Something must be wrong."

"It could be a mix-up," I said. "Maybe it was someone else who emailed Hudson, someone with a similar name."

"Let me check." Hudson pulled out his phone, scrolled through his emails, and showed the screen to my grandmother.

"Well, that is Martha's email address." Grandma read the email, then her eyes widened. "Hang on a minute, what's this at the bottom about her will?"

"Martha wants me to come see her on Monday to discuss leaving her estate to the library," Hudson said. "We had a gentleman at my old library do something similar. It was a lovely gesture. When he passed away a few years later, we were able to purchase some new computers in his name."

"Um, if Martha does leave the library her estate, you'll be able to buy more than a few computers," I said. "She's one of the richest women in the state."

Hudson's jaw dropped. "Oh ... okay, so not similar at all."

"This makes no sense. Everyone knows that Martha's niece will inherit. That's been set in stone for years. She wouldn't suddenly change her will." Grandma locked eyes with me. "Thea, you need to go with Hudson on Monday and find out exactly what's going on with Martha. I'm worried about her."

"Don't worry, we'll get to the bottom of it. I'm sure the book donation and the will are a misunderstanding on both counts," I said.

I squeezed my grandmother's arm to reassure her, but I wasn't sure it helped. Martha had a reputation for being a shrewd businesswoman and a meticulous record keeper. She wasn't the kind of woman who would impulsively change her will. And she certainly wasn't the type to donate her precious books to the library. Grandma was right—something was off.

* * *

"I'm going to call some of the gals from my book club and see if they know anything about Martha." Grandma pointed to the boxes of books that Martha had supposedly donated. "Why don't you go through those and see what's inside? Maybe it's just old magazines."

As Hudson cleared space on one of the tables, I looked around for Cassidy, but she had disappeared. I picked up the box cutter, then asked Hudson which one he wanted to start with.

"How about this one?" Hudson hoisted a carton which had originally contained canning jars onto the table. It reminded me of the sauerkraut Martha canned every year. When she distributed it during the holidays, people joked that it reflected her sourpuss personality. For the most part, it was good-natured teasing. But there was an undercurrent of truth beneath the comments. Martha was grumpy on a good day. Catch her on a bad day and she'd give you a tongue-lashing you wouldn't easily forget.

I removed the packing tape, then opened the box. "This doesn't look like old magazines."

"But they are old." Hudson pulled out a dark green leather-bound book. It had gilded pages, and the cover was embossed with an intricate leaf pattern.

When Hudson opened it and inspected the cover page, his eyebrows shot up. "This was published in the nineteenth century. By the looks of it, I'd say it's a first edition."

"It says volume one on it. Looks like it's part of a series," I said before grabbing some of the other books from the box. They also looked like antiques. A dead moth floated out from between the cream-colored pages of one of the dust-covered volumes, and the smell of old paper wafted through the air.

"Do you think they're valuable?" I asked Hudson.

"I couldn't say for sure," he said. "But by the looks of it, they're probably worth something to a collector."

"They all seem to be related to gardening," I said, removing the rest of the books from the box and stacking them gently on the table. "Ray would be interested in these. He collects old books about plants."

Hudson gave me a questioning look. "He's the president of the Garden Club, right?"

"That's right. He claims to have the greenest thumb in the county," I said. "Actually, he and Martha are super competitive when it comes to who grows the best flowers. Last year, Martha won the blue ribbon at the county fair. Ray was livid. He claimed Martha didn't comply with the entry regulations and should have been disqualified."

Hudson chuckled. "Sounds a bit like my Aunt

Nancy. She's big on rules and regulations."

"I think Martha had Ray disqualified from some other competition before that. Those two excel at playing tit for tat." I glanced at Martha's other boxes. "I'm curious what's inside those."

"Only one way to find out." Hudson cleared some more space, before we sorted through the contents. Two of the boxes contained gardening-related books, and the other three were an assortment of classic literature and cookbooks.

"Gelatin salad, yuck." Cassidy had reappeared holding a collection of vintage North Dakota recipes. She wrinkled her nose. "Especially with pineapple and shredded carrots mixed in it."

"Don't knock it until you try it," I said.

Cassidy set the cookbook down gingerly, as though it might be contagious.

"I might have to pick this one up." Hudson held up a copy of *Brave New World*. "Have you guys read it?"

"Does it have dragons in it?" Cassidy asked.

"Um, I don't think so," Hudson said.

She shrugged. "I only read books with dragons in them. Although, I usually wait until the movie's on one of my streaming services."

I didn't have the heart to tell Cassidy that books were way better than TV or film adaptations. I'm not sure she'd understand the difference. Instead, I turned to Hudson. "I read it. You gotta love a good dystopian novel."

"Maybe I'll pick this up at the book sale," Hudson said. "That is, if Martha really is donating these books."

"Except for the cookbooks, most of them look valuable, especially the gardening ones," I pointed out. "If she really does want to part with them, this probably isn't the best way. The highest we ever price a book is five dollars."

Hudson nodded. "Yeah, you're right. She could probably get a fortune for some of these."

Cassidy inched closer. "How much do you think they're worth?"

"*The Thirteen Problems* by Agatha Christie recently sold at auction for over sixty-three thousand dollars," Hudson said. "And someone paid almost a quarter of a million for Arthur Conan Doyle's *The Hound of the Baskervilles.*"

Cassidy's eyes widened. "No way."

"It's true. They were part of Charlie Watt's estate." When Cassidy gave him a blank look, Hudson added. "You know, the drummer from The Rolling Stones."

"I wonder if that's why they went for so much," I mused.

"Could be," Hudson said. "The auction would have generated a lot of attention because of whose estate it was."

Cassidy ran her hand across the stacks of books. "It's crazy to think people would pay so much money for these old, dusty things."

"Like I said, I don't know how much these are worth." Hudson held up his hands. "Some of them might be worth a few hundred dollars. Maybe. Or maybe more."

"We should probably put them back in the boxes," I suggested. "And keep them locked up until we know what Martha wants to do with them."

"I can do that," Cassidy offered.

"Thanks," Hudson said. "Thea, can you help me with pricing these over here?"

While Hudson and I were sorting through a pile of children's books, my grandmother came back into the meeting room.

"You'll never guess what Geraldine told me," she said, her forehead creased with worry. "She ran into Martha at the doctor's office last week. Geraldine's bunions have been causing her a lot of trouble. I keep telling her she needs to stop wearing those pointy shoes, but she—"

"Can we talk about Geraldine's footwear another time?" I interjected, not wanting my grandmother to go off on a tangent about arch support and adequate toe room. "What did she say about Martha?"

My grandmother raised her eyebrow. "Martha told Geraldine that she was going to donate her estate to the children's hospital in Bismarck."

"Not the library?" Hudson asked.

"She didn't say anything about the library to Geraldine." Grandma took a step closer to us, then lowered her voice. "And that's not all. Two days before that, Martha told someone else that she was going to leave everything to the Veterans' group."

"All great causes," I said. "Is she planning on splitting her estate among all of them?"

"No idea," my grandmother said. "But whatever she's planning, it doesn't seem to involve Sharon."

"Sharon Voight is Martha's niece," I explained to Hudson before turning back to Grandma. "I wonder what Sharon has to say about all this."

"Someone should talk to her." My grandmother gave me an appraising look. "It's been a while since you've had your hair cut."

I pulled my long blonde hair around the nape of my neck and looked at the ends. "I suppose I could use a trim."

"This is quite a change of topic." Hudson chuckled. "We've gone from Martha's will to haircuts."

Grandma grinned. "Sharon is a hairdresser. She and her husband own the Beauty Bucket."

"Oh, I get it now," Hudson said. "You're sending Thea undercover to question Sharon."

"Let's not get carried away," I said. "I'm not planning on interrogating the poor woman. We want to find out if her aunt's okay, that's all. It'll be easier to get Sharon to confide in me if I'm getting my hair done."

My grandmother nodded. "Sharon loves to talk about herself when she's got someone in her chair."

"What time are you seeing Martha on Monday?" I asked Hudson.

Hudson checked the calendar on his phone, then said, "I have to cover the front desk until eleven, so I told her I'd come by after that. Does that work for you?"

"Sure. I can pick you up." I tucked my hair back behind my ears, and said, "I'll see if I can get an appointment at the Beauty Bucket for late Monday afternoon. It'll probably be better to chat with Sharon after I've seen her aunt."

Grandma nodded as she looked around the meeting room. "What did you do with Martha's books?"

After explaining that Cassidy was boxing them back up, I told my grandmother some of the books looked valuable.

"Uff da," Grandma muttered.

"How's it going over there?" Hudson asked Cassidy.

Cassidy was on the other side of the room, shoving something in her backpack. She gave Hudson a faint smile. "Fine. I put Martha's boxes out of the way in the corner. I gotta go now."

"I was about to order pizza," Hudson said. "And Rose baked some cookies."

"Sorry, my sister is picking me up." Cassidy slung her backpack over her shoulder.

"No problem," Hudson said. "Will we see you again tomorrow?"

"Do I have a choice?" Cassidy asked glumly.

Hudson cleared his throat. "Um, that's between ..."

"Don't worry, I'll be here," Cassidy called as she walked toward the door.

"Be sure to sign the time sheet in my office before you take off," Hudson said.

After Cassidy left, I asked, "What was that about?"

"Nothing." Hudson waved a hand in the air. He smiled at my grandmother. "You should take a look at the books Martha donated."

"*Supposedly* donated," Grandma said as she followed Hudson over to where Cassidy had stacked Martha's boxes.

"There's one that I think is a first edition." Hudson sat on the floor and started sorting through the books. "Hmm, I don't see it."

"Which one are you looking for? The green one?" I crouched down next to Hudson.

After doing a thorough search of all the boxes, Hudson and I looked at each other.

Hudson frowned. "It seems to be missing."

"And not just that one," I said. "Some of the others are gone, too."

"That can't be." Hudson started searching through the boxes again.

"What the heck?" I muttered under my breath. Right before Cassidy left, I had seen her tuck something into her backpack. Could it have been the books? The same books that Hudson said might be worth a bit of money.

CHAPTER 2
A VERY OBNOXIOUS CHAMELEON

The weekend went by quickly. Between volunteering at the library during the days and catching up on work in the evenings, I was worn out.

My grandmother had finagled help from a few more people, which was a relief, especially considering Cassidy and Ray never came back. We managed to make headway sorting through books and pricing them, but there was still a huge amount to do in order to be ready for the book sale. By the time Monday morning rolled around, I never wanted to see another book again.

Well, that wasn't exactly true. There were some books I was desperate to see again—the ones belonging to Martha, which had gone missing. Hudson and I had searched the meeting room several times over the weekend. Hudson had called and texted Cassidy repeatedly to see if she knew anything about them. But she never responded. Hudson certainly wasn't looking forward to telling Martha her books had disappeared.

Putting that worry out of my head for the time being, I took care of some administrative tasks for a few hours. After a mid-morning cup of coffee and Danish with my grandmother, I headed to the library to pick Hudson up for our visit with Martha.

As I drove down the gravel road leading from my grandparents' farmhouse toward town, I thought about how lucky I was to have my own consulting business. I had spent too many years trying to climb the corporate ladder in Minneapolis. The backstabbing at the previous company where I'd worked was beyond belief, finally driving me to quit my job, move back to North Dakota, and take charge of my own career.

I specialized in organizational development, which was a fancy way of saying that I helped companies be more effective. The work I did for my clients was wide ranging. One day it might be leadership coaching, the next I could be working on strategy development and employee engagement. And there was always the never-ending administrative stuff to take care of. Being my own boss had a number of advantages—the ability to work remotely and having a flexible schedule topped the list.

Of course, there were also downsides. I missed having colleagues to chat through things with and an assistant to lighten the load. Being the sole employee could be lonely. That was one of the reasons why I enjoyed volunteering at the library—it was a chance to connect with other folks. And, if I'm honest with myself, a chance to spend time with Hudson.

Since Hudson had moved to Why, we had solved a murder along with my grandmother, discovered a shared love of mid-century furniture, and entered an ax throwing competition together (we took third place). It was safe to say he was quickly becoming a good friend. Friends are good. I could always use more friends.

I was so lost in thought that I almost missed the turnoff to the library. Pulling into the parking lot, I realized I was twenty minutes early. My grandmother would be proud. She had lovingly cross-stitched her mantra, 'If you're not ten minutes early, then you're late,' and hung it next to the kitchen clock, a not-so-subtle reminder to get a move on.

Rather than wait for Hudson in the car, I popped into the library to look for something new to read. My nightstand was already piled with an assortment of non-fiction titles, a couple of thrillers, and a volume of poetry. But can you really ever have too many reading options? It's important to be prepared for whatever literary mood might strike.

When I walked inside the library, Hudson was at

the front desk, scanning returned books into the system. He looked up from the computer and gave me a quizzical look. "Is it eleven already?"

"No, I'm early. I'm going to check out the new releases while I wait."

"Actually, there's a new display of library staff picks you might want to check out," Hudson suggested. "It's in the Collingsworth Wing."

I nodded. "Sounds good. See you in a bit."

As I walked through the library, I smiled at a toddler attempting to pet a large, fluffy black and white cat. One of Hudson's conditions of employment was that his cat, Dr. McCoy, would be able to accompany him to the library. The feline was a huge hit with the patrons, especially the kids.

Dr. McCoy meowed at me as I passed and rolled over onto his back, allowing the toddler to stroke his belly. It was adorable.

When I walked into the Collingsworth Wing, I saw the display Hudson had mentioned on a table to my right. It was hard to miss. A large sign saying 'Let Our Staff Pick Your Next Read' was tacked on the wall. The letters were slightly crooked, and someone had drawn a picture of Dr. McCoy in crayon in the corner. No doubt the kids in one of the Saturday Crafternoon sessions had played a part in making it.

Underneath the sign, books were propped up on stands on the table. Attached to each book was a card indicating which staff member had recommended it and why. My eye was immediately drawn to Hudson's pick—*Tomorrow, and Tomorrow, and Tomorrow* by Gabrielle Zevin. On his card, Hudson had written:

This is a powerful story about enduring friendships. Set in the fascinating world of video game design, it will leave you pondering your own 'game of life.'

Underneath that, Hudson had included a quote from the book:

It's tomorrow, and tomorrow, and tomorrow. It's the possibility of infinite rebirth, infinite redemption.

It struck a chord with me. Hudson and I had both experienced deep loss. I had lost my parents at a young age, and he had lost his wife and unborn child. It was the hope and promise of all the tomorrows ahead of me that kept me going. Perhaps it was the same for Hudson.

Not wanting to spiral into dark thoughts about losing loved ones, I turned my attention back to the book. I examined the cover in more detail. The title was written in a typography reminiscent of old video games. Gaming had never been my thing unless you counted building houses in *The Sims* or playing word games on my phone.

"Why does the phrase 'tomorrow, and tomorrow, and tomorrow' sound familiar?" I muttered to myself.

As I was pondering, there was a sudden whooshing noise accompanied by a bright flash of light. I groaned, recognizing it as a sign that the most annoying creature I had ever encountered in my life had just arrived on the scene.

Yep, there he was. Edgar, a chameleon that only I had the 'honor' of being able to see, sat perched on top of one of the books on display.

Edgar had first made an appearance several months ago, shortly after I had discovered a dead body at the library. In the beginning, I thought I had been hallucinating. Though after confiding in my grandmother, she told me Edgar was my guide, sent to help me by some mysterious force in the library.

However, I disagreed. Edgar's idea of helping was to belittle me, complain about living in North Dakota, and constantly demand hot dogs. Just because all the other women in my family had animal guides, it didn't mean I wanted one. I did just fine on my own, thank you very much. Anyway, if the library was going to foist a guide on me, why couldn't it have been a sweet angora rabbit like my grandmother had?

Of course, I only had Grandma's word to go on. I couldn't see her guide, and she couldn't see mine. Yet another frustrating quirk of our library. Mysterious, magical forces weren't really my thing.

My grandmother was adamant that all of my female ancestors adored their guides. I most certainly didn't share that sentiment.

After looking around to make sure no one was in earshot, I turned and glared at Edgar. "What are you doing here? Shouldn't you be off catching flies somewhere?"

Edgar rotated one of his strange, beady eyes in my direction. The other one was looking at goodness knew what.

"Believe me, lady, I'd rather be anywhere than here," he said, his thick, raspy New York accent grating on my every nerve. If you closed your eyes and listened to his voice, you'd swear the speaker was an 80-year-old chain smoker from Brooklyn, not a colorful reptile.

I tried it. I closed my eyes, hoping that maybe this time when I opened them back up, there'd be a guy who had been an extra on *The Sopranos* standing in front of me.

Nope, didn't work. The only thing in the vicinity was a chameleon. Super. Just what every girl needs in her life, an obnoxious reptile.

"Listen lady, clearly, you need my help," Edgar continued. "So, here I am. I don't make the rules."

I put my hands on my hips. "But I don't need your help."

"You do when it comes to Shakespeare."

I smacked my forehead. "Right, that's what it is. 'Tomorrow, and tomorrow, and tomorrow' is from *Macbeth*."

"Bingo!" he exclaimed.

"I'm surprised you know Shakespeare."

"Why? Because I'm a chameleon?" Edgar flicked his tongue out angrily. "You think we're illiterate? Is that what you're saying? I'm just a dumb reptile, is that it?"

My eyes widened. I wouldn't have pegged Edgar as the sensitive type. "Listen, I wasn't implying that you can't read. But all you ever talk about is how crappy you think the hot dogs are in North Dakota. Shakespeare plays, not so much."

"Well, they are crappy," he huffed. "The hot dogs, I mean. Not the Bard's masterpieces."

I rolled my eyes. "Then why are you always demanding that I bring you a nacho dog from Swede's diner?"

"Because that's the only way I can choke down one of your so-called hot dogs ..." Edgar paused for a moment to belch loudly. Do all chameleons burp or is it just this particular one? I had no idea. Then he continued, saying indignantly, "The toppings help disguise the taste."

"Listen, I really need to get going," I said. "Hudson and I are going to see—"

"Visit that batty old lady, yeah I know."

"You mean Martha? How do you know that? And that's not very nice, by the way, calling her batty."

"You and the dweeby library guy were talking about it yesterday in the meeting room," Edgar said. "Take a little bit of advice from me, lady. Maybe you don't need to yell all the time. Your voice carries."

"I wasn't yelling," I argued, conscious that I had raised my voice. Glancing around again to make sure no one could hear me, I leaned forward and hissed, "Tell you what, you stay out of my business, and I'll stay out of yours."

"Fine by me," he said, shrugging his scaly shoulders.

I clutched *Tomorrow, and Tomorrow, and Tomorrow* to my chest and spun around. As I started to walk away, Edgar called out, "Hey, princess! Check out the books shelved under 615. Specifically, 615.9, I have a feeling you're going to find that subject interesting."

"I don't take reading advice from you," I huffed. "And, before you ask, no, I'm not bringing you back a nacho dog."

* * *

Hudson grinned when he saw what book I was checking out. "Great choice, if I do say so myself."

"Hopefully, it lives up to expectations," I teased. As I tucked the card with Hudson's handwritten recommendation inside the copy of *Tomorrow, and Tomorrow, and Tomorrow*, I asked, "Ready to get going?"

After letting the library staff know that he'd be back in a couple of hours, Hudson grabbed his coat. When we reached the lobby, he held the front door open for me. Once he stepped outside, he squinted in the bright sunlight. "I hope this weather holds up until next weekend so that we can have the book sale outside."

"Plan for the worst and hope for the best," I said, parroting a saying my grandmother had cross-stitched on a throw pillow at home.

"That's a good motto. I should put it on a sticker. Speaking of, I don't think I showed you these yet." Hudson reached into his messenger bag and pulled out a die cut sticker of a buffalo standing on top of a stack of books. "I thought I could sell these at the book sale as a part of the fundraiser."

"People will love them." I was in awe of his creativity. I didn't have an artistic bone in my body, unlike Hudson. He not only designed his own stickers, but also printed and cut them.

"Here, this one's for you." But before Hudson could hand the sticker to me, the town's resident buffalo raced through the library parking lot, skidding to a stop in front of us.

"I don't think I'll ever get used to this," Hudson said as the large creature nuzzled against him. "This has to be the only place in America where a buffalo casually strolls the streets looking for handouts and snuggles. I can't imagine anything stranger than that. Can you?"

I resisted the urge to tell Hudson that until you've seen a talking chameleon from New York City who offers you unsolicited advice, you haven't really experienced strange. In comparison, a needy buffalo making himself at home in our town was perfectly normal.

Reaching over to scratch the large shaggy creature behind his ears, I asked, "Does that feel good, Bufford?"

Hudson wagged a finger at me. "That's not his name, and you know it."

"It will be once the results from the contest are in." The buffalo nudged me like a cat would, making it clear I needed to continue scratching. I switched to his other ear and apologized. "Sorry, buddy." Then I looked back up at Hudson. "How many entries are there so far?"

"Lots," Hudson said. "We had to get a second box for more people to put their entry forms in."

I grinned, thinking about the absurdity of it all. A buffalo had adopted our little town, and everyone was eager to give him an official name. I had been glad my choice of moniker—Bufford—made the top ten options that people had to choose from. Now, I was crossing my fingers that enough people agreed with me that it was the perfect name.

"Announcing the contest results at the end of the book sale was a genius idea," I told Hudson. "Half the town will probably show up."

"That's what I'm hoping for," he said. "It'll be good publicity for the library."

"Okay, that's enough scratches for today," I said to the buffalo. "We need to get going."

After giving me a reproachful look with his large brown eyes, the shaggy creature sauntered off in the direction of the bowling alley. I smiled to myself, imagining him pushing a bowling ball down the lane with his nose, and snorting loudly when he got a strike. Not that it was going to happen. Most business owners drew the line at letting the big fellow inside their premises. Not that he didn't try.

Hudson and I got into my car and headed toward Martha's farm. As we drove past freshly plowed fields, Hudson said, "I've never been out this way. It's pretty."

"Really? You've been here for months."

"I haven't had much spare time since the move. There's been a lot to get up to speed with my new job." Hudson turned his head to look at the tractor I had just passed. "You know, the Larsens will be back from Arizona in a few weeks. They said I can stay in their guest room until I find a new place to live, but I'm sure they'd like me gone as soon as possible."

My heart sank. I had become accustomed to Hudson renting the house across the road from us. He was at my grandparents' place as much as he was at the Larsen house. Now, I'd have to go out of my way to catch up with him.

"Have you had any luck? There's not much available to buy around here, let alone rent." My knowledge was based on my half-hearted attempt at looking for a place of my own. When I came back to

Why from Minneapolis, I had moved in with my grandparents, and I was reluctant to leave. While they were only in their late sixties, who knew how much time they had left? I was cherishing our moments together.

"I think I found something," Hudson said. "It's in town. A converted garage apartment. Cat friendly, too."

"What does Dr. McCoy think about moving? It'll be smaller than the Larsen house."

"He'll be fine for now. One of these days, I want to build my own place. That was something my wife and I always talked about doing," Hudson said, his voice cracking slightly.

I murmured sympathetic noises before turning into the entrance to Martha's farm.

We passed a large barn desperately in need of some fresh paint, a couple of old corrugated metal silos, several dilapidated sheds and outbuildings, and a disused chicken coop. With all of Martha's money, you would have thought she could have kept things in better shape.

"Wow, this place is huge," Hudson said. "How does Martha manage it all?"

"What you're seeing is just the tip of the iceberg," I said. "Martha owns a lot of acreage. She leases most of it. Some of it to farmers, and some of it to the oil companies. I don't think she has any wind turbines on her land, but I could be wrong."

I parked in front of the sprawling two-story house, then pointed at a more modest structure to the right. "That's the Sunflower Cottage. The farmhands used to live there. Grandma said that's where Martha's nurse stays now."

As I got out of my car, an old rusted pickup truck barreled down the drive, kicking up gravel and dust. I scowled when it screeched to a halt next to me. I had two nemeses in my life. One was a more recent acquaintance—the annoying chameleon. The other was of the human variety—Bobby Jorgenson, a deadbeat who had been picking on me since we were kids.

"Hey there, Thea," Bobby said as he hopped out of his truck, a cigarette hanging from his mouth. "Glad I ran into you. Can you lend me some money? I'm almost out of smokes."

I arched an eyebrow. "Seriously? You want me to give you money, so you can buy cigarettes?"

"Well, yeah. No need to get all high and mighty. It's not like I'm asking you to buy me beer or nothing."

"Why don't you get a job?"

"Already have a job." He pointed at the flower beds and greenhouse next to the house. "You're looking at the new gardener."

"You're working for Martha?" I asked incredulously.

"You betcha. It's a pretty good gig, too." Bobby

scratched his head. "Except payday isn't until next week."

I jerked a finger at the garden beds. "Well, payday may never come unless you actually, you know, work."

"Um, Thea, maybe we should go," Hudson suggested.

Bobby shrugged, took one last puff of his cigarette, and tossed it on the ground.

I narrowed my eyes as he crushed it with his boot heel. "Really? You're just going to leave your cigarette butt there?"

"Nice seeing you, Thea," Bobby called over his shoulder as he ambled over to the greenhouse. "If you change your mind about the loan, you know where to find me."

"I can't believe Martha hired him," I said. "The longest Bobby Jorgenson has held down a job is probably three weeks, and that's only because the foreman at the fertilizer plant felt sorry for him."

"Maybe Bobby turned over a new leaf," Hudson said.

"Yeah, right."

Hudson shrugged, then said, "There's the lady who dropped off Martha's books on Friday."

A woman with dark auburn hair was standing in the doorway of the Sunflower Cottage, waving at us. She was dressed casually, wearing jeans and a striped sweater. "Did you come to pick up another donation from Martha?" she called out.

"Not exactly," Hudson said as we walked toward the woman. "I think there's been a misunderstanding."

I held out my hand and introduced myself. "Thea Olson. It's nice to meet you. I'm helping Hudson out with the book sale."

"Audra Bordey," she replied, her accent just as Hudson had described—soft and musical. "I'm Miss Lund's new nurse."

"How are you finding North Dakota?" I asked, always curious to know what folks thought of the Peace Garden State.

Audra gave me a warm smile. "It's beautiful. Very different from where I grew up though."

"Where was that?"

"An island in the Caribbean called Saint Marie. It's a British Overseas Territory," Audra explained. "I came to the States a couple of years ago."

"Ah, so you spell 'center' with an 're' instead of an 'er' at the end," I said.

"And we put unnecessary 'u's in our words like your Canadian neighbors," Audra joked. "But there's also a big French influence on the island, so we make up for our British spelling with baguettes and fabulous wine. You should visit. It's warm year-round. Perfect for a winter escape."

"That does sound nice," I said. "Winters can be brutal here."

She nodded. "I know. I worked in Bismarck before this assignment. I was always wrapped up in a thick duffle coat, hat, scarf, and even two pairs of gloves. It still wasn't enough to keep the biting cold and wind out. I think my blood is too thin."

"Tell me about it," Hudson said. "I'm originally from Florida."

"Yes, one winter was enough for me." Audra chuckled. "That's why I'm looking at other positions back in the Southwest. I can stand the heat, but not the cold."

I cocked my head to one side. "So, this is just a temporary assignment?"

"They all are," Audra said gently. "It's hard when your client only has a few months left to live, but that's the job."

"Wait a minute, are you saying Martha is terminally ill?" Hudson asked.

"I thought you knew that already. That's why Miss Lund wanted to see you about her will." Audra's eyes widened as she pressed her lips together. "Please don't tell anyone what I said. I can't afford to lose this job."

My jaw dropped. When my grandmother had asked me to visit Martha and find out what was going on, I'm sure the last thing she expected for me to report was that the poor woman only had a few more months to live. Things made more sense now, although for a very tragic reason.

CHAPTER 3
SO MANY BOOKS

After letting it slip that Martha only had a few more months left to live, Audra clammed up, refusing to divulge any details about Martha's illness. Once she went back inside the Sunflower Cottage, I shot Hudson a horrified look.

"Wow, just wow. Poor Martha ... I can't believe Audra won't tell us what's wrong with the poor old lady," I said. "Do you really think she'd lose her job if she spilled the beans?"

"The more important question is how Martha is doing." Hudson ran his fingers through his hair, mussing up his curls. I resisted the temptation to smooth them down. His curls were sticking up at odd angles, but in an incredibly adorable kind of way.

Hudson took a deep breath, and then exhaled

slowly. "It can't be easy knowing your time on the planet is quickly running out."

"Well, it does explain a lot," I said softly. "Changing her will, donating her books, even hiring Bobby Jorgenson."

"Bobby? How do you figure that?"

"Martha isn't a lady who suffers fools. And Bobby is a Class A fool." I zipped my jacket, and jammed my hands in my pockets. It might be sunny out, but the constant breeze gave a slight chill in the air. Springtime in North Dakota could be unpredictable when it came to the weather. You could get sunshine, rain, or snow, sometimes all of them at the same time.

Perhaps I was shivering for another reason, though. The news about Martha dying was a lot to absorb. I wrapped my arms around myself. "Maybe her illness is affecting her mentally, and she's forgotten what an idiot Bobby is."

"If she's not mentally competent, we shouldn't be talking to her about her will," Hudson pointed out. "Agreed?"

"Actually, I don't know if that's the case. It was just speculation on my part. She could still be sharp as a tack. Maybe? Gosh, I don't know." I looked back over at the Sunflower Cottage, wishing Audra would have told us exactly what was wrong with Martha, so that we were better prepared.

"Let's get this over with." Motioning for Hudson to follow, I walked toward the main house. My hand hovered over the doorbell. Instead of pressing the button, I turned back to Hudson. "Remember how my grandmother and I said Martha was a hoarder? I mean, um, a collector."

"Yeah."

"Well, prepare yourself," I said. "It's been a few years since I was here, but I can't imagine it's gotten any better."

Hudson smiled. "That sounds mysterious."

"The mystery is how anyone can live like this," I said as I rang the doorbell. "There was this other gal I knew who had so much stuff crammed in her mobile home that you could hardly breathe. I wonder what drives people to keep collecting things?"

Hudson chuckled. "Whatever you do, don't look at my sticker collection."

"Really? That many?"

"You have no idea."

I smiled, and rang the bell again. Maybe Martha was taking a nap. I was about to knock when a woman's voice called out from a speaker mounted next to the door. "Come in. I'm in the kitchen."

When I pushed the door open, Hudson gasped. "Wow. This is ..." His voice trailed off as he surveyed the front hallway. Books were stacked against both walls, all the way to the ceiling. The entryway table was piled high with old *National Geographic* magazines. The stairway caught his eye, leading to the second floor. But it was nearly impassable because of the old encyclopedia sets lined up on the risers. A children's picture book even balanced precariously on the banister.

"And I thought it was bad before," I muttered under my breath. Martha took being a bibliophile to the next level.

"Which way to the kitchen?" Hudson asked.

As I led him down the hallway, I kept my arms close to my body, worried that brushing against the multiple stacks of dusty books would cause them to tumble down. Being buried underneath an avalanche of paper seemed like a horrible fate. Would a search and rescue team be needed to dig us out?

The kitchen was in a little better shape, but not by much. At least there was a bit of diversity in the clutter here, as Martha's books competed with other objects for space. A basket full of Scandinavian troll dolls sat on top of the stove, the counters were crowded with vintage jadeite dishware, and Christmas ornaments were hanging from the exposed rafters. Based on the appearance of this room, Martha's interior decorating style could be summed up as 'rustic bookish mishmash.'

Martha was sitting at an oak dinette set positioned in a breakfast nook by a large bay window. The heavy brocade drapes were drawn back, providing a view out to the garden beds, which, much to my surprise, Bobby Jorgenson was weeding.

"There you are," Martha said. Two dogs were

snoozing at her feet—Pomeranians from the look of them—and a purring gray tabby cat sat in her lap. The older woman looked much the same as the last time I had seen her—short white hair permed into tight curls, clear gray-blue eyes, and red patches on her skin from a long-standing battle with rosacea. "How are you, Freya?"

"I'm Thea," I corrected her. "You must be thinking of my cousin."

"Uff da." Martha squinted at me. "Of course. Freya is the one who married the butcher fellow, isn't that right?"

"Yes, that's right, ma'am."

"Remind me again, what's your husband's name?" Martha waved a hand in Hudson's direction.

"Oh, we're not married," I said quickly.

Martha stared at Hudson for a beat, and said, "You better put a ring on this girl's finger before she gets away."

"Hudson isn't my boyfriend," I spluttered, as my cheeks grew warm.

"Now, listen here, young man," Martha said firmly. "Freya is a nice girl."

"Thea," I reminded her.

"That's what I said," Martha snapped. "Thea is a nice girl. You can't treat her like some floozy."

Hudson bit back a chuckle. "You can be assured that I have the utmost respect for Thea. We're just friends, nothing more. But there's no romance going on here. Isn't that right, Thea?"

I smiled and nodded in agreement, but inwardly my stomach sank. Telling yourself that you'd only ever be friends with a guy was one thing. Hearing him say it out loud was another.

Martha glared at Hudson. "Humph!"

Humph, indeed.

"Sorry, I should have introduced myself earlier. I'm Hudson Carter, the new library director. We've exchanged a few emails."

"Right, about my will." Martha motioned at her walker. "Be a dear and move that out of the way so you can sit down."

Hudson cleared his throat. "If we're going to discuss your will, perhaps it would be best if we met with your lawyer, or your ... doctor."

"My doctor? He's fine when it comes to blood pressure medicine, but he doesn't know the first thing about legal documents." Martha rubbed her hands together. "But before we get down to business, I think we should make some muffins to go with our coffee. Lisa tells me I shouldn't use the oven when she's not here, but it will be our little secret."

"Who's Lisa?" I asked.

"You know, the blonde girl who helps me around the house."

I furrowed my brow. "Wait ... Do you mean Audra? Your nurse? She has auburn hair."

"Audra. That's what I said. Maybe *you* need to see

the doctor," Martha said to me, her tone acerbic. "He can clear that wax out of your ears. Now, grab that recipe box from the shelf over the sink."

It wasn't hard to spot it nestled among the spice bottles and plastic food storage containers. The gorgeous rosemaling decorative painting on the sides made it stand out. I smiled as I read the inscription on the top. I had studied Norwegian in college for a few years and was pretty sure *hemmelige oppskrifter* meant 'secret recipes.'

After I set the box on the kitchen table, Martha told me to get some butter out of the fridge.

"Is there anything I can do to help?" Hudson asked.

Martha pushed the recipe box toward him. "Look through these and see if you can find the recipe for ricotta chocolate chip muffins."

I looked over Hudson's shoulder as he sorted through the contents of the recipe box. He set a bunch of folded up pieces of paper and old brown envelopes to one side. I picked up one of the envelopes and admired the ornate handwriting on the front. "Did you do this with a fountain pen?"

"Yes, I always use fountain pens," she said. "I don't like the feel of ballpoint pens."

I examined the envelope more closely, wondering about the recipe hidden inside. "What kind of dish is 'Tagetes Patula Lund?' Is it Spanish?"

"It's none of your business," Martha said sharply.

"So, these really *are* secret recipes," I noted,

putting the envelope back on the table.

When Hudson took too long to find the recipe Martha wanted, she grumbled, "Just look for the one that says, 'From the Kitchen of Rose Olson' at the top."

I asked, "Oh, you're making my grandmother's muffins?"

"Yes, but with a twist. Instead of chocolate chips, I use crushed up croutons and add a splash of sauerkraut juice for zing."

"Well, that certainly is a twist," I said, reminding myself not to sample her baking. Sauerkraut was okay on hot dogs, but definitely not meant for muffins. But I didn't tell Martha that. When you don't have long to live, people should humor your idiosyncrasies, even if that included adding sauerkraut juice to muffins.

Martha glared at me. "Where's the butter? We don't have all day, missy."

I sighed. Illness certainly hadn't tempered the older woman's infamous mean streak. "Coming right up," I said pleasantly.

When I tripped over one of the dog toys scattered on the floor and stumbled into the fridge, Martha slammed her hand on the table. "Stop being so clumsy, Freya."

"It's Thea," I muttered under my breath.

After I picked up the magnets I had knocked off the door, I opened the fridge. Inside were the usual things you'd find in a fridge—orange juice, milk, cans of pop, and … books. So many books. I finally found a few sticks of butter behind a volume of poetry.

"Maybe we should make muffins later," I suggested, taking a seat across from Martha. After repositioning my feet so that they weren't in the Pomeranians' way, I added, "I had a big breakfast, and I know Hudson had some things he wanted to discuss with you."

Martha started to argue with me, but Hudson jumped in. "Thea's right. We should talk about the books Audra dropped off at the library on Friday."

The older woman narrowed her eyes. "What books? Who is Audra?"

"Audra is your nurse," Hudson reminded her. "She thought you wanted to donate them to the book sale. You did mention them in your email to me."

"Nonsense. I would never give away any of my collection." Martha pulled a pile of books that had been sitting on the side of the table toward her protectively. The dark green antique leather binding and gilded pages reminded me of the books that had been in the boxes Audra had dropped off at the library. "You need to bring them back. Immediately."

"Of course. I can bring them by tomorrow. There's just one problem ..." Hudson rubbed his hands together nervously.

I gave Hudson a warning look. How would Martha react if we told her some of her books were missing? Would the stress of knowing her prized, seemingly valuable, possessions had disappeared be too much given her illness?

"What's the problem, sonny?" Martha snapped.

"Everything's fine," I said. "What Hudson is trying to say is that one of the boxes got a little dinged up. That's all."

When Hudson nudged me under the table, I covered my mouth with my hand and said quietly to him, "We'll track down Cassidy and get the books back."

"What are you two lovebirds whispering about?" Martha's voice softened as she smiled at us.

"Your will," I said, uttering the first thing that popped into my head.

Hudson shot me a look as he said in an undertone, "I thought we weren't going to talk about that."

"My will," Martha said brightly. "That's a good idea. I wish I had thought of it."

"I really think you should talk to your lawyer about this," Hudson said. "You wouldn't want to do anything hasty."

"Don't be ridiculous. It's really quite simple. The lawyer draws up the paperwork and I sign it."

"You change your will often?" I asked.

"You betcha. I started doing that recently. It keeps people on their toes."

"What about your niece?" I asked. "I thought the two of you were close."

"Sharon?" Martha stroked the cat on her lap thoughtfully. "Well, I suppose you're right. She should get something. Do you think she'd like a set of encyclopedias?"

"Um, sure," I said.

"Which one should I give her?" Martha asked. "I have an *Encyclopedia Britannica* from 1964 or how about a set of *Collier's*? The *Collier's* has nice color photos in it."

"Oh, I don't know. It's hard to say," I said.

"Good point. I'll give her both," Martha said.

We chatted for a few more minutes on a bewildering range of topics—who was going to win the World Series this year, the correct ratio of sugar to water for hummingbird feeders, and Martha's favorite sauerkraut recipe.

As Hudson and I got up to leave, Martha grabbed my hand. She had a surprisingly firm grip. "Can you stay for a few minutes, Thea? There's something I need to talk with you about."

Hudson nodded. "I'll meet you at the car."

Martha waited until she heard the front door open and close before she leaned toward me. "Someone is trying to kill me. You need to stop them."

* * *

The cat on her lap began growling, as if to underscore the elderly woman's pronouncement that someone wanted to murder her. Martha shushed the tabby. "Don't worry, Astrid. Thea is going to stop the killer."

I shifted uncomfortably in my chair. "Why do you think someone is trying to kill you?"

"Because I'm rich, sweetheart." She waved a hand toward the large bay window. "I inherited all this land from my daddy when he died. At the time, everyone said that there was no way a woman could manage such a big farm on her own, but I showed them."

"Remind me, when did your father pass away?" I asked.

"It was a long time ago. I had just turned twenty-five. I never married, so I was still living at home. My mother had passed away a few years earlier. I think my daddy was heartbroken. He couldn't bear to keep living without her," Martha said, her eyes growing moist. But then her tone turned bitter. "It didn't help when my good-for-nothing brother got in trouble not long after. When Teddy got locked up, it was the last straw. Daddy cut Teddy out of his will and had a fatal stroke days later."

I made a mental note to ask my grandmother about Teddy. I knew that he had been the black sheep of Martha's family. Other than the fact that he had fathered two children—Sharon and her brother Robert—I didn't know anything else about him.

Martha looked off into the distance, a faint smile on her lips. "You should have seen all the fellows who tried to woo me the instant I inherited the farm. But I said no to each and every one of them. If I wasn't good enough for them before I was rich, I didn't want them after."

I studied the woman. She looked more lucid than before. I couldn't put my finger on exactly what was different, but something was. Had it all been an act earlier?

Martha told me to put the electric kettle on and make her a cup of coffee before we continued our conversation. "Use some of that instant stuff in the canister by the microwave. If you put enough sweetener in it, it's not so bad. Make some for yourself too."

An assortment of mugs sat on the windowsill over the sink. As I selected one with a penguin holding an umbrella for Martha and one with a cat reading a book for me, I hoped Hudson wasn't getting bored waiting for me. After scooping coffee crystals into each mug, I added boiling water and gave them a good stir. When I brought the steaming mugs over to the table, Martha asked me to pass her the sugar.

"No, not that one. That's for company," Martha said when I brought over a glass container with sugar cubes in it. "The other one. My secret sweetener. No one is allowed to use it but me. I only have a limited supply."

It took a couple of trips back and forth to the table before I selected the right one—an enameled metal container with a decorative yellow flower pattern which said 'Candy' on it.

"That's my idea of a little joke. The stuff is sweet, but it doesn't have any calories." Martha opened the container and pulled out a glass bottle. It seemed odd to stash the bottle within the metal container, but this whole visit had been strange. The older woman continued; her voice hushed as though she was worried someone would overhear us. "It's a new kind of sweetener, made from root vegetables. You can only get a hold of it if you have special connections. I've been trying it out. Still thinking about if I want to replace regular sugar with it permanently."

Martha poured a healthy amount of the sugar substitute into her coffee. She put the lid back on the bottle firmly, as if to let me know it was off limits, and looked at my mug. "You can have some of those sugar cubes if you want. Or there's a bottle of regular sweetener on the counter over there."

I couldn't be bothered to get back up from the table. "No, that's okay."

After Martha took a sip of her coffee, she said, "So, where were we?"

"We were talking about how men wanted to marry you for your money. Do you think that's why someone is trying to kill you?"

"Given my age, I don't think it's a jealous lover," Martha said wryly. "So, the motive could be money or revenge."

"Why revenge?"

Martha shooed the cat off her lap, and leaned

forward. "I've made a lot of enemies in my time. It was the cost of doing business back then, much like it is now."

I furrowed my brow. "But why would someone wait until now to try to kill you over a business deal?"

"That's a fair point," Martha said. "See, I knew there was a reason why I picked you for this job."

"What job?"

"We already discussed this, Thea." Martha drummed her fingers on the table. "You're going to find out who is trying to kill me and stop them."

"This is a job for the police, not me," I said, holding up my hands.

"I don't trust the new chief of police. She isn't from around here." Martha pursed her lips. "It's too bad your brother didn't get the job. Leif might be young, but he's a local boy."

I was at a loss for words. When the previous chief of police had been put on administrative leave and later fired, my brother had assumed the acting chief of police role. While Leif enjoyed running the department on an interim basis, it had been a stretch for him, given his relative inexperience. So, it hadn't been a surprise when the mayor hired someone else to take on the role permanently. But I knew it stung Leif's pride to be back on the beat.

"Leif says the new chief is very competent," I said to Martha. "If you're concerned that someone wants you dead, then you really should speak with her.

There isn't anything I can do for you, honestly."

"Don't sell yourself short. You've solved two murders, correct?"

I rubbed the back of my neck. "Um, kind of."

"That's two more than the new chief has solved." When I gave Martha a questioning look, she said sharply, "I know how to use a computer. I did my due diligence. The woman simply doesn't have the experience that you do."

My phone beeped. Hudson had texted, wanting to know if everything was okay. Yeah, not really. I was sitting at a kitchen table with a woman who was convinced someone was going to take her life before her illness did. And what made it worse was that she wanted me to solve the crime before it happened.

Letting Hudson know I'd be out shortly, I turned back to Martha. Maybe the best thing to do was humor her, and let the police know what she had said. So, they could take the appropriate course of action.

"Okay, you believe someone is trying to kill you," I said. "Do you have any idea who it is?"

"I have a few ideas, but I'm not ready to divulge that information yet," she said cryptically. "But if I were you, I'd consider the obvious—book collectors and family, not necessarily in that order."

"Right," I said slowly. "Is there any other information you're able to share?"

"I can tell you how they're trying to do it."

"Well, that's a start," I muttered. When Martha

didn't elaborate, I asked, "How exactly are they trying to kill you?"

"Poison," Martha said simply. "Someone has been slipping something into my food."

"How do you know that?"

"Because of my symptoms." Martha ticked them off one by one for me. "Shortness of breath, nausea, stomach problems, skin issues, and chest pain."

I reached out for Martha's hand and gave it a gentle squeeze. "Don't you think that could be because of your illness?"

She snatched her hand away. "Maybe you're not as bright as I thought you were. Needing a hip replacement doesn't give you those kinds of symptoms."

"What does your doctor say?" I asked, ignoring her jab.

"I want you to start with Audra," Martha said. "She used to prepare all my meals. It could be her."

"Audra is your nurse. Why would she want to poison you?"

Martha frowned. "I don't know, but she's the only person who could be putting poison in my food."

"You said she *used* to cook for you? When did that change?"

"A few days ago. Once I realized what was going on, I got smart and ordered a bunch of frozen meals online. That's all I eat now. The cheese enchilada is my favorite. That reminds me, I should stock up on some more while they're on sale." She scrawled something on a notepad with her fountain pen, then looked back up at me. "Why are you still here? Go get started on the investigation."

As I left the kitchen, I shook my head. What in the world was going on? Was Martha's life really in jeopardy? Or was her illness causing her imagination to run wild?

CHAPTER 4
HAIR DYE NUMBER 42

When I walked out of Martha's front door, I felt like I was in a different world. The sun was shining brightly, Bobby Jorgenson was stretched out under a tree asleep, Hudson and Audra were chatting by the greenhouse, and there weren't piles of books stacked everywhere. Everything appeared normal.

I turned and looked back at the house. Inside, things were far from normal. There was a woman who was convinced someone was poisoning her, and she insisted that I find her would-be killer. What more, she wanted me to start my investigation with her new nurse Audra.

Well, that wasn't exactly what was going to happen. Instead, I was going to let the police know what Martha had said. They could do an investigation.

More than likely, they'd come to the same conclusion as me. It was sad, but the truth of the matter was that Martha's symptoms were probably consistent with whatever illness she had, not the result of someone putting poison in her food.

But as I walked toward Hudson and Audra, I felt a sense of disquiet. What if Martha wasn't imagining things?

"Everything okay?" Hudson asked. "What did Martha want?"

"I think she just wanted to chat," I said, not wanting to get into what Martha and I had really discussed in front of Audra. "Old people get lonely."

Audra smiled. "It was nice of you to spend some time with her. She likes it when we play card games or I read to her after dinner, but it's good for her to have other visitors."

"Dinner? Do you cook for Martha?" I asked, remembering what Martha had said about only eating pre-made meals she purchased online.

"Of course. In addition to my nursing duties, I also take care of her other personal needs such as bathing, meals, driving her to doctor appointments, that sort of thing." Audra chuckled. "Miss Lund sure does take offense to the fact that the DMV took away her driver's license."

"So, she doesn't eat frozen meals?"

Audra arched an eyebrow at me. "Certainly not. I serve fresh, home-cooked meals. Speaking of which, I need to get to the grocery store and pick up some fruit and vegetables."

"It was good chatting with you," Hudson said. "Don't forget to swing by the library and get a temporary resident card, so you can borrow books."

"I'm not much of a reader, but I appreciate the offer," Audra said. "And apologies again for bringing those books to the library. I was sure Miss Lund said she wanted to donate them."

"It's not your fault," Hudson said. "She said in her email to me that she wanted to give some books to the library. If Thea and her grandmother hadn't told me how attached Martha was to her collection, I wouldn't have thought anything of it."

Audra tugged the bottom of her sweater, inching it down over her ample hips. "She has so many books as it is, you would think she could get rid of a few. But elderly folks get set in their ways."

"The important thing is that Martha doesn't get stressed worrying about her books," Hudson said. "I'll bring them back tomorrow."

I said a silent prayer that we would find the missing books before then. Why was a small town, so Cassidy Dahl couldn't be that hard to track down.

When we got into the car, I asked Hudson if Audra had said anything about what was wrong with Martha.

"No, she still feels bad about telling us Martha is terminally ill. She made me swear not to tell anyone."

Hudson rolled down his window, and added, "Audra seems like a capable nurse. I'm sure Martha is in good hands."

"That depends on who you ask." I started laughing. It was a slightly hysterical laugh, a reflection of how bizarre the situation was. "According to Martha, Audra is trying to poison her."

Hudson sighed. "Dementia is awful, isn't it?"

"Do you think that's what it is?"

"Maybe it isn't dementia, but something's not right. She kept mixing you up with your cousin, Freya," Hudson reminded me. "I suppose that could have been from cataracts. But our conversation with her was a bit, um, odd."

"As horrible as it is to say, dementia would be the simplest explanation," I said. "A murderer with their sights on an old terminally ill lady? Not so much."

* * *

After I dropped Hudson off, I sat in my car in the library parking lot and called my brother. Leif was on patrol, so I relayed my conversation with Martha to the desk sergeant. After being assured the police would look into Martha's fears that she was being poisoned, I breathed a sigh of relief.

My hair appointment wasn't for forty-five minutes. Since blue skies were still out, I left my car at the library and walked to the Beauty Bucket. As I cut through the town square, I noticed our resident buffalo munching on some of the primroses by the bandstand. The parks department wasn't going to be too happy about Bufford's choice of snack.

When I pushed the door to the salon open, I was greeted with the harsh smell of chemicals, a reminder that hair treatments and manicures came at a price. The place was completely deserted. Some small businesses in Why struggled to stay afloat, and with the opening of a new glitzy hair place on the other side of town, I imagine Sharon's business was hurting.

"What can I do for you, hon?" the woman behind the front desk asked brightly as she snapped her gum. She had glossy black hair pulled back into a tight ponytail, and her bright red lipstick matched her fingernail polish. "Did you want me to touch up those roots of yours?"

I patted the top of my head. "Roots?"

"Don't worry. I'll have you looking like a million bucks in no time. Your boyfriend will thank me." As the woman came around the front desk and examined my hair, I tried to place her. Was she a new transplant in town? Having lived in Minneapolis for so many years meant that many of the new residents were strangers to me. "Let's see, I think number forty-two is the closest match."

"Forty-two?"

She blew a bubble, then said, "That's the shade of hair dye you use, right?"

I tucked my hair behind my ears and took a step back. "This is one hundred percent natural. I've never dyed my hair in my life."

"Huh. It's not often you see a woman in her forties with natural white blonde hair." She winked at me. "Don't worry. Hairdressers are like lawyers. We don't reveal what our clients tell us in confidence. You can continue to pretend this color is natural, and I won't say otherwise."

"I'm twenty-nine, not forty," I said.

"Oh, if you say so." She handed a smock to me. "Why don't you put this on while I mix up the hair dye? I'll be back in a jiff."

"Is Sharon here?" I asked. "I have an appointment with her to get my hair trimmed. *Not* colored."

"No, she's off for a few days. Family emergency. But I can squeeze you in."

Shivers ran down my spine. "What kind of emergency? Is Sharon's aunt, okay?"

"Martha? As far as I know, she's fine," the woman said. "Sharon has some issues to deal with closer to home if you know what I mean. Lots of drama going on."

While I was interested in the nature of Sharon's personal drama, I didn't want to spend another minute in the presence of this gal. She was eyeing me up like I was a discarded Weird Barbie who needed to be saved.

"I'll reschedule my appointment for another time,"

I said as I inched toward the door.

"I wouldn't count on Sharon being in the best shape to do your hair. When you're stressed out, accidents can happen with scissors. You wouldn't want to end up with an accidental bob." The woman handed me her card. "Tell you what, if you change your mind, give me a call and I'll put you on my schedule. We can also talk about doing a little Botox. It'll take years off you. You don't want your boyfriend to trade you in for a younger model, do you?"

"No thanks, um …" I glanced down at the card and stifled a laugh. Never had a name better suited someone than this. "No thanks, Artifice."

When I finally managed to escape Artifice's clutches, I practically ran out of the salon. I needed to get away from this place that preyed on women's insecurities, convincing them that they needed to change themselves in order to be loved and accepted.

Thankfully, the Bookish Nook was right next door. I couldn't think of a better way to soothe my frazzled nerves than a visit to Why's only bookstore which also doubled as a café. The aroma that greeted me was completely different from the Beauty Bucket. Instead of harsh chemical smells, the heavenly scents of dark roast coffee and freshly baked pastries filled my nose. The artful displays of books and the cozy seating areas created a warm and inviting atmosphere that made customers want to linger.

"Hey, Thea. I haven't seen you here in a while."

George, the owner of the Bookish Nook, was pouring some cream into a ceramic pitcher. He set it next to a container of sugar on the counter before he straightened up a stack of napkins. "Are you looking for anything in particular, or just browsing?"

"Just browsing," I said. "I was next door at the Beauty Bucket and thought I'd stop in."

"Nice haircut," he said, his soft Southern accent betraying the fact that he wasn't originally from these parts.

"I didn't get my hair done," I said.

"Oh, well, it looks good anyway." He gave me a sheepish smile. "Artifice is always telling me I should come in for a makeover. I don't know why, though."

I could imagine Artifice being unimpressed with George's sense of style. He wore his long frizzy hair back in a ponytail, his beard was patchy in spots, and his faded jeans, sandals with socks, and long-sleeved t-shirt screamed bookish nerd rather than a man about town.

"I don't think you should change a thing," I said, not sure if I was talking more to myself than to George. "Be you, unapologetically."

George beamed. "That means a lot coming from you."

Yikes. Now I was worried that I had given him the wrong impression. Quickly changing the topic, I said, "Do you know what happened to Sharon? Artifice said she's away dealing with some family issues."

"I saw her before she left. Poor thing was crying her eyes out." George leaned forward, ready to gossip. "Her husband ran off to Bozeman with the receptionist from the salon. He's demanding a divorce from Sharon so he can marry this other girl. Poor Sharon went out there to try to talk him out of it."

"Oh, wow, I had no idea. That's awful."

"Yeah, and what makes it worse is that Sharon isn't going to have a penny to her name once the divorce goes through."

"Really?"

"North Dakota isn't a community property state," George explained. "When a couple divorces, their property is divided equitably, not equally. And while both terms start with 'eq,' they don't mean the same thing. Trust me, I know. When my wife divorced me, she got the lion's share of our property. I was lucky to keep the bookstore."

"I guess I had no idea how it worked."

"Well, I hope you never do," George said. "Can I get you a coffee?"

After ordering a hazelnut latte, I asked how long Sharon and her husband had been married.

"Four, or five years? It was a second marriage for both of them. From what I understand, he owned everything. So, the nice house, car, her fancy clothes, and the vacations they took to Hawaii ..." George made a magician's *poof* motion with his hands. "It's all gone. Vanished forever."

George turned his attention back to the espresso machine. After pouring hazelnut syrup and steaming milk into a cup with two shots of espresso, he pointed to the service area on the counter. "Napkins and sugar are over there. I've also got a sugar-free sweetener, if you prefer. It's this new stuff made out of rutabagas. I know the guy who makes it. He ships a big batch to me wholesale. I repackage it and sell it to a few private customers. You should try some and tell me what you think."

"No, I'm good. The hazelnut syrup is sweet enough." While I waited for my latte to cool, George and I chatted a bit more about the financial impact of Sharon's impending divorce. "Well, at least she has the salon to fall back on," I said.

"Nope, not even that. Her husband owns the business. Sharon is an employee. I bet you anything once the divorce is final, he fires Sharon and promotes his new wife from manning the front desk to head stylist. She's always been miffed that Sharon wouldn't overlook the fact that she hadn't completed cosmetology school and only let her work as a receptionist."

"Wow. I can't even begin to imagine what Sharon must be going through."

"Yeah, it's a lot. But she'll get through it," he said philosophically.

I fixed my gaze on George, wondering what other gossip he knew. "Hey, have you heard anything about her aunt Martha?"

George scratched his head. "Not much, other than the fact that she changed her will a few weeks ago. She cut Sharon out. Another reason why the poor girl is in such bad financial shape."

"Yeah, I can see that," I said. "She must have counted on inheriting from her aunt. It wouldn't have mattered about her husband owning the bulk of their assets."

George gave me a knowing look. "I heard Martha's leaving all her money to a dog rescue organization instead. Maybe I should adopt a dog? Or maybe a cat who could hang around the bookstore like that one at the library? What do you think?"

"You can't go wrong with a cute cat or dog," I said.

"If I was really lucky, Martha would leave me all her books," George said. "Now, that would be a dream come true."

Our conversation was cut off when a customer came in wanting help finding a memoir someone had recommended. All he knew was that the title was written in red letters and it was about cannibals set on an island somewhere.

George puzzled over this for a moment, then raised his hands in victory. "I know exactly what you're talking about—*The Sex Lives of Cannibals Adrift in the Equatorial Pacific*. It's very funny. Follow me. We have a copy in the back."

As George went to locate the memoir, I thought

about the similarities between booksellers and librarians. They both helped folks find their perfect book. Sure, the former did it for profit and the latter as community service, but the more people who helped nurture a love of reading in the world, the better as far as I was concerned. George was one of the good guys.

I grabbed my coffee cup and waved goodbye to the bookseller, leaving with more to puzzle over. It sounded like Martha had definitely cut her niece out of her will, otherwise Sharon wouldn't be so worried about her husband divorcing her and leaving her penniless. But why? What had happened between Martha and Sharon that would have led to such a drastic action?

* * *

As I was leaving the Bookish Nook, my grandmother called, asking if I could meet her at Swede's Diner. It was already after four. I had been planning on heading back home and doing some work. But after the visit with Martha, the personal ambush at the hair salon, and my chat with George, I was feeling overwhelmed. I'd have to catch up on my to-do list later.

When I walked into the diner, Norma, the feisty red-headed waitress who had been working there since I was a kid, shoved a menu in my hand. "The special is sauerkraut patty melts served on pumpernickel bread. Tell Swede your order and help yourself to coffee."

"Uh … When did this become a self-service joint?" I asked.

"Since now." Norma untied her apron and flung it on the hostess station. She grabbed her jacket from the coat rack, and yelled over to the kitchen, "I'm leaving!"

Swede pushed the kitchen door open and scowled in Norma's direction. "Whaddya talkin' bout?" The short, balding man looked confused. "You had a break twenty minutes ago."

Norma marched back over to the kitchen and glared at her boss. "I'm not going on break, you moron. I'm leaving for good."

"Huh?"

"I don't like the way you treat me!" Norma barked.

Swede scratched his head. "But I don't treat you any differently than before."

"Exactly," Norma said before storming out.

The entire restaurant had gone silent during their exchange. But the minute the front door slammed shut behind Norma, the place began buzzing with conversation. Most folks were eager to dissect Norma and Swede's fight. Others wondered who was going to serve their food. Swede had been short-staffed as it was, with only Norma working this shift. Now Swede was all on his lonesome.

Swede still stood by the kitchen, looking dumbstruck. He was used to Norma sassing him. But she had upped her game to a new level, leaving him in a lurch with a restaurant full of hungry customers.

I looked at the menu I was clutching in my hand. My stomach grumbled, reminding me I hadn't eaten anything since this morning. Taking a few cautious steps in Swede's direction, I said, "Can I get a chicken salad sandwich with some fruit salad on the side?"

Swede tilted his head to look up at me. "Do I look like a waitress to you?"

"Um, not exactly. But Norma said to place our orders with you."

He narrowed his eyes. "Then you'll have the special."

"But I'm not really in the mood for sauerkraut."

"Tough. You wanna eat? You're gonna eat sauerkraut. I got a case of it in the storage room that I need gone."

As the kitchen doors swung closed behind Swede, my grandmother tapped me on my shoulder.

"Sorry I'm late, dear. Your grandfather needed help in the barn. He got some more twine." Grandma looked around the diner. "Where's Norma?"

"I'll tell you about it when we sit down," I said. "By the way, I hope you like sauerkraut."

After telling Swede to add another special to my order, I led the way to a table that had just opened up near the window. We were lucky to snag it. Even without a waitress, the diner had continued to fill up with hungry customers. And most of the folks who had been here when Norma and Swede had their spat were still lingering, eager to gossip about what had happened.

Once we were seated, I filled my grandmother in on Norma's dramatic departure, then told her about Martha's illness.

"Oh, my goodness." Grandma pressed her hands together and closed her eyes. I watched her lips move, no doubt saying a silent prayer for Martha. She cleared her throat, and asked, "How long does she have left to live?"

"I don't know. Audra didn't give us any details." I paused mid-story to tell a couple to place their order with Swede in the kitchen. Then I turned back to my grandmother. "On top of all that, Martha thinks someone is trying to poison her."

Grandma's eyes widened. "Poison? She didn't really say that, did she?"

"She was adamant about it. And—here's the crazy part—she wants me to investigate."

"On your own? Doesn't she know about the 'Three Investigators?'" Grandma joked.

I smiled at my grandmother's reference to Hudson, her, and me. Several months ago, the three of us had worked together to solve a murder. We had dubbed our gang of amateur sleuths the 'Three Investigators' after the classic children's detective series. Hudson was even talking about making some stickers to commemorate our partnership.

"This seems more like a case for the police," I said. "I passed along the information to them."

"You don't think someone is really trying to kill Martha, do you?"

I shook my head. "No, not *someone*. Just whatever horrible disease she has."

"Hang on a minute. You had your hair appointment with Sharon earlier. Did you tell her about what her aunt said?"

"That's a whole other story," I said. "Let me grab us some coffee first."

When I went up to the coffee station, one of the other patrons was already brewing a fresh pot. "Let me fill those cups up for you," she offered. "I'm no Norma, but I can manage that at least."

"Be careful before Swede puts you to work," I warned her. "I'm not sure how long he can cope without Norma."

My grandmother was grabbing a pitcher of cream from a neighboring table when I walked back. "Your grandfather isn't here, so we can add as much of this to our coffee as we want."

"It'll be our little secret." I took a sip of my milky brown coffee and sighed contentedly. "He doesn't know what he's missing."

"Thor is too stubborn to try something new. He's always drunk his coffee black, and he always will."

"Did you see the look Grandpa gave Hudson the other day when he was talking about the new raspberry truffle mochas at the Bookish Nook?"

"Fortunately, Hudson is a good sport and your grandfather seems to like him." Grandma added a splash more cream to her cup, and waved to someone behind me. "You'll never guess who just walked in."

I twisted in my seat and saw Doc Thomson standing by the hostess station, patiently waiting for Norma to appear.

The doctor was one of those men who stood out in a crowd. Not because he had movie star looks, but because he was nearly seven feet tall. He'd played basketball as a freshman at the University of Minnesota in the late eighties. But after injuring his ankle in a freak accident involving a goat and a corn maze, his days on the court were over. So, he buckled down in class, got into medical school, and had been the town's physician ever since he graduated. He had a warm bedside manner, but it was his willingness to dress up in outlandish costumes at community events in order to amuse the kids which made him one of the town's most popular residents.

"Go ask Doc to join us," my grandmother said. "Maybe we can find out more about Martha's situation from him."

After I ushered the doctor over to our table, Swede rang the bell in the kitchen. "Order up. Two specials," he called out.

"Think those are ours?" I asked my grandmother.

"Probably," she said. "Do you mind grabbing them? Get something for Doc while you're up there."

The doctor gave me a quizzical look when I walked behind the counter. "Are you waitressing now?"

"For the time being," I said. "What can I get you?"

"Just some coffee and a piece of pie. Rhubarb if they have it."

After setting the two plates of sauerkraut patty melts on a tray, I turned back and called out through the service window, "Doc wants some rhubarb pie."

Swede flipped a burger over on the grill, and pointed at me with the greasy spatula. "Tell Doc there ain't any more rhubarb. Only apple."

I grabbed a slice of apple pie from the pastry cabinet and added it to the tray. After a quick stop at the coffee station for the doctor, I carefully walked back to the table, trying not to spill anything in the process. Norma made it look so much easier than it was.

"Doc told me something very interesting," my grandmother said as I set the plates down. "Martha had a huge argument with her niece a few weeks ago. She hasn't spoken to Sharon since."

"George said the same thing. It's awful when family falls out." I slipped into my seat, and scraped the sauerkraut off of my patty melt. "Considering she doesn't have long to live, you'd think Martha would want to reconcile with Sharon."

"Exactly how long does Martha have to live?" Grandma asked Doc pointedly.

Doc wiped some crumbs from his mouth, before he shook his head. "You know I can't answer that. Patient confidentiality."

I shoved the unwanted sauerkraut to the side of my plate. "Did you know Martha thinks someone is trying to poison her?"

Doc sighed. "Sometimes—hypothetically speaking —people can imagine things when they're suffering from ..."

"Suffering from what exactly?" my grandmother prodded. "Hypothetically speaking, of course."

"I've said too much already." He wagged a finger at her before grabbing his phone from his jacket pocket. "Hang on, I need to get this."

While Doc had a hushed conversation, I took a few bites of my patty melt. Unfortunately, it still tasted like sauerkraut. Maybe some ketchup would help. But before I could grab the bottle from the other side of the table, the doctor said something to us which made me forget all about masking the taste of fermented cabbage.

"I've got some bad news," he said soberly. "Martha is dead."

CHAPTER 5
BRING YOUR FAMILY TO WORK DAY

"Martha's dead?" I stared at Doc Thomson, my eyes wide with shock. "That's not possible. I saw her a few hours ago. She was very much alive."

My grandmother set her coffee cup down slowly. "What was she sick with? Did that kill her?"

Doc held up his hands. "Even though Martha has passed, the rules about patient confidentiality still apply. But what I can say is that she was living on borrowed time. Although I wouldn't have expected her to go so soon ..." He pushed his plate of half-eaten pie to the side. "It could have been a heart attack or a stroke. Anyway, we'll see what the postmortem has to say."

"Who was that on the phone? The EMTs?" I asked, curious about what had transpired.

"Her nurse Audra called me," Doc said. "She found Martha in the kitchen and tried to revive her, but to no avail."

"Martha was lucky to have been able to afford a full-time nurse," I mused. "I'm not sure most health insurance plans would cover something like that."

"Her niece insisted on it," the doctor explained. "Martha didn't want someone living in the house and being a nuisance. But she kept forgetting to take her medicines. She was also struggling with everyday tasks given her bad hip. Sharon kept badgering her, and Martha finally agreed to have a nurse. But her caveat was that the nurse stay in the adjoining cottage and leave her alone as much as possible."

"You said Martha and Sharon had a falling out," my grandmother said. "Was that what it was about?"

"I don't think so," Doc said. "I heard about it from Martha's previous nurse, Lisa. She didn't go into details. All she said was that she had overheard Martha and Sharon arguing about money before Sharon stormed out of the house."

"What happened to the previous nurse?" I asked.

"Martha fired her," Doc said dryly. "They were lucky the agency could get a replacement so quickly."

"Martha did have a habit of firing people," my grandmother said. "Most folks didn't live up to her standards."

I shook my head. "Makes you wonder why she hired Bobby Jorgenson to do her gardening. The only standards he lives up to involve drinking beer and bumming cigarettes."

"Uh, he made her laugh," Doc said. "Don't underestimate the power of laughter when you're sick."

While Doc and my grandmother reminisced about Martha, I stared at the pile of sauerkraut on my plate. Martha would never can another batch of sauerkraut to hand out as holiday presents again. Sauerkraut had taken on a whole new meaning now.

A familiar voice interrupted my train of thought. "You look like you ate something that disagrees with you, Thea. Should I avoid the special?"

My baby brother stood by our table, his posture as stiff as his crisp police uniform. Looking at him was like staring in a mirror—we both had white blond hair with pale blue eyes like our grandfather and a lanky build like our grandmother. Unlike Leif, my hair was long, my ears were pierced, and I had a tendency to slouch.

"You can finish mine if you want," I said to Leif.

"Nah, that's okay. I just came in to get some coffee to go," Leif said. "They need to do something about the coffeemaker at the station."

"Maybe the new police chief will get you guys one of those fancy machines that makes espresso and lattes," I said.

"Yeah, right." My brother flashed me a cocky grin as he snatched some fries off my plate. When some of the ketchup landed on his shirt, he groaned. "Darn it. I just washed this."

"*You* washed it?" I pointed at our grandmother. "I think you mean your laundry service took care of it."

Leif rolled his eyes at me, grabbed a napkin, and dabbed at the spot. After making more of a mess than he started with, my brother gave up and wandered off for a while to chat with a friend. When he came back to our table, he stole my remaining fries. They were cold by this point, so I didn't care. Not that I told him that.

Before I could pretend to be angry about the fries, Leif's phone buzzed. He grabbed it out of his pocket and listened intently. Then his eyes widened. "Martha Lund was poisoned. Are you sure?"

* * *

"Slow down," I said as Leif made a sharp turn onto Main Street. Intellectually, I knew that people would get out of our way when they heard the police cruiser's siren and saw the flashing lights. But we were going awfully fast. "Martha's already dead. No need to add anyone else to the casualty list."

"Hey, I got top marks in my law enforcement driving course. You're in safe hands." My brother shot me a look before turning his attention back to the road. "Besides, the chief said to get there on the double. She's not going to be too happy when she sees you tagging along."

"She'll understand. It would have been rude to say no to your older sister." I gripped the armrest as Leif made another sharp turn. "Anyways, I have critical information about Martha's murder. She told me that someone was trying to poison her. The chief will want to hear all the details of our conversation personally."

"I never said she was murdered," Leif said. "I said she had been poisoned. Big difference. She probably took something accidentally. Folks were saying Martha had been confused lately."

Thinking about how clear-headed Martha had been when it was just the two of us talking earlier today, I said, "I'm not so sure about that."

Leif grunted in response.

"What's the new police chief like?" I asked as we tore past the Little Pickle grocery store.

Leif considered this for a moment, and answered, "She's hard to read."

"It can't be easy for you," I said. "You were acting chief of police for months, only to have the mayor give the job to someone else."

"It is what it is," Leif said as he pulled into Martha's driveway. "Besides, this town needs someone with more experience in the top job."

Leif parked his cruiser near the coroner's vehicle. From what I understood, the county coroner only came out on site when there were questions about how someone had died. No surprise really, since I had reported Martha's fears that someone was trying to poison her. I had lots of questions as well.

I unbuckled my seatbelt, grateful that I didn't need it to save my life during the harrowing ride over to Martha's home. I said, "I'm impressed. You're taking this well, unlike when you didn't win class president in the ninth grade. You moped around the house for weeks."

Leif punched me in the arm playfully.

"Ow!" I cried. "That hurt."

"Did not."

"Did too."

For a moment, I was transported back to road trips with our grandparents. Leif and I would be in the backseat arguing while my grandmother threatened to make us shelve books in the library as punishment if we didn't shape up. I chuckled as the memories flooded through my mind, although my expression sobered as another police cruiser pulled in beside us.

As I got out of the car, I noticed several officers from the Why police force, along with a couple of deputies from the county sheriff's office, in a huddle by the greenhouse. There sure were a lot of law enforcement officers on site, casting doubts on Leif's theory that it had been an accidental poisoning. Especially since they had all arrived so quickly after Audra discovered Martha's body.

I tensed when the police chief marched briskly toward us. Even though the chief was barely five feet tall, her compact frame was well muscled, and she exuded an aura of confidence that was frankly intimidating. I had never met the woman before, but I knew from articles in the local newspaper she had been on the professional wrestling circuit prior to a stint in the Air Force. I was starting to regret my impulsive decision to hitch a ride with Leif.

"What took you so long, Olson?" Chief Jeong barked at my brother.

"Um ... there were some cows loose," Leif stammered. "I had to slow down to get around them."

The chief stared at Leif for a few moments, before she turned her gaze in my direction. "And you are?"

"Thea Olson." I held out my hand. "It's nice to meet you."

Chief Jeong ignored my attempt to greet her with a handshake. As I awkwardly lowered my hand, she said, "Olson, huh? I already have an Olson here. Why would I need another one?"

"Thea is my sister," Leif said.

"Is the rest of your family on the way?" the chief asked. "Are they bringing a picnic? How nice of you to organize a family reunion on my watch."

Ignoring her sarcasm, I took a step forward and squared up my shoulders. "This is not Leif's fault. I didn't give him a choice about bringing me."

"Oh, right, that's because it's 'bring family to work' day. I completely forgot," Chief Jeong said.

"No, it's because I have information about Martha's death."

The other woman considered this for a moment and said, "I'm listening."

After telling the chief about my conversation with Martha earlier in the day, I said, "So, you see, Martha was convinced that someone was trying to poison her. Your desk sergeant said the police would look into it."

Chief Jeong scowled. "Is that it?"

"Um, yeah." I looked down at the ground, suddenly feeling like a five-year-old talking about their imaginary friend to a disbelieving adult.

"Go wait over there." The chief pointed toward the Sunflower Cottage, and then spun around to face Leif. "You, go down to the gate by the road and make sure no other unauthorized individuals enter the property."

I slinked away, feeling sorry for having put my brother in the doghouse with his new boss.

Audra was standing in her doorway, surveying the scene. When she saw me, she beckoned me over. "I didn't know you worked for the police."

"I don't," I said.

"Oh, you're with the coroner's office."

"Nope."

"So, you're here because ..."

My stomach clenched. I couldn't really tell her the truth. Saying 'I'm here because Martha had thought you might be trying to kill her, and you were at the top of her list of suspects' wouldn't really fly. Instead, I said, "I've helped the police in the past with murder investigations."

It was a half-truth. If you asked the police, they would have labeled my assistance as 'meddling.' Even my brother would have said the same thing. But without my so-called meddling, two killers might have gotten off scot-free.

Audra clutched her chest. "Murder?"

"Yeah, but I don't know for certain that Martha was murdered," I admitted.

That was a true statement. My gut told me someone had killed the poor woman. But our justice system seems disinclined to accept hunches as evidence. So, I'd have to prove it, digging around and finding something that would stand up in court. Of course, it would help if I knew who did it. That was always a good starting point.

I studied Audra's reaction. She looked genuinely shocked by the possibility that Martha had been murdered. Or maybe she was a good actress.

"I understand you alerted the authorities after discovering Martha was dead," I said.

"That's right. I found her lying on the kitchen floor when I went in to administer her afternoon medications. I tried to revive her, but it was hopeless ..." Audra took a deep breath. "Do you mind if we go inside? I think I need to sit down."

I followed Audra into the cottage. A small hallway

led into a combination living-dining space. On one side of the room was a large trestle table with benches, on the other was a comfortable-looking leather couch and two recliners surrounding a stone fireplace. The walls were bare except for a dried wreath hanging over the mantelpiece. Lavender, sunflowers, and other dried flowers were nestled among wheat stalks and some sort of foliage with long, narrow leaves. The effect was stunning.

Audra gave me a shy smile. "I made that."

"Really? It's gorgeous. My grandmother would love it."

"I sell them at farmers markets and craft fairs in my spare time," she said. "Well, I used to. I haven't had much time for that kind of thing lately."

"Do you dry the flowers yourself?"

"No, I buy them online." Audra led the way into the kitchen. "Since I move around so much from assignment to assignment, I don't generally have a place where I can hang flowers to dry."

As Audra sank into one of the kitchen chairs, I surveyed the room. Pine cabinets, a farmhouse sink, and a cast-iron stove gave the room a homey look. Metal canisters and stoneware crocks were perched on shelves, and glass jars of dried herbs lined the butcher block counters.

"Sorry, I'm being a bad hostess." Audra got to her feet. "I should be offering you something to drink."

This was hardly a social visit, but I wouldn't say no

to a cup of coffee. The adrenaline that had been coursing through my system since finding out about Martha's demise had dissipated, and a caffeine fix would help.

When I said as much to Audra, she gave me an apologetic look. "Sorry, I only have herbal tea."

I smiled. If I hadn't known that Audra originally hailed from the Caribbean, tea would have been a dead giveaway that she wasn't from these parts. Folks out here drank coffee non-stop. When guests stopped by, the first thing you did was brew a pot of the stuff.

"Water's fine," I said.

After setting a glass of tap water on the table for me, Audra filled up the tea kettle and set it on the stove to boil. Next, she pulled one of the glass jars toward her and scooped a generous amount of dried leaves into a teapot. "I make these tea blends myself. This one is a special mix, great for soothing frazzled nerves. You sure I can't interest you in trying a cup?"

"No, thanks," I said. "I'm fine with water."

When Audra joined me at the kitchen table, I asked, "Do you mind telling me what happened when you found Martha?"

"Sure. I went into the house to bring in the groceries when I found her. The poor dear must have collapsed when she tried to get up. I was always telling Miss Lund to use her walker, but she didn't like it." Audra gave a wry smile. "Said it made her feel like an old lady. She was a feisty one, that's for sure."

"What time did you find her?"

Audra put her hands around the ceramic teapot as though to warm them. "Around a quarter after four."

"Had you seen Martha before that?" I asked.

"I saw her earlier in the morning …" Audra paused to pour some tea into a strainer which she had set on her cup. "I gave Martha her medications as normal, and fixed her a snack. After I did the dishes, she dismissed me. She wanted to prepare for the meeting she had with you and the library director."

"Okay," I said, mentally drawing up a timetable. "You saw Martha in the morning, then you left. What time did you say that was again?"

Audra eyed me warily. "I didn't say. But it was around ten."

"Sorry, it's a personality quirk of mine. I like to organize things in my head."

"Occupational hazard, I guess." When I gave her a quizzical look, Audra added, "Working with the police."

"Um, yeah. Anyway, Hudson and I arrived around twenty after eleven and left around noon after speaking with you. You were heading out yourself to run errands, right?"

"That's correct."

"Was it normal to leave Martha alone for that long?"

Audra pressed her lips together. "What are you implying?"

"Nothing," I said quickly. "Like I said, it's just how my brain works."

The other woman relaxed slightly. "Sorry, it's a lot to take in. Even though I'm used to my elderly patients passing away, it's still hard to lose one of them."

Deciding to press my luck, I asked, "Can you tell me more about when you found Martha?"

"Well, it was clear that she had been dead for several hours. And when I saw ..." Audra's voice trailed off at the sounds of people arguing outside. "I wonder what's going on?"

I pulled back the lace curtain, peered out the kitchen window, and grinned. "It looks like my grandmother is here and she's having a few words with the new chief of police." I kind of felt sorry for Chief Jeong. Grandma was not someone you wanted to go head-to-head with, especially if it involved the possible murder of a friend of hers. If anyone were going to bet on the outcome of this little match-up, you'd be wise to back my grandmother.

CHAPTER 6
ANGER MANAGEMENT ISSUES

Later that night, Grandma, Hudson, and I had a Three Investigators meeting in my grandparents' kitchen. Hudson had brought Dr. McCoy with him, and the large, fluffy cat was snuggled on my lap, purring loudly. As I shifted slightly in my seat, taking care not to disturb the cat, I surveyed the warm and homey room. My grandmother had recently been talking about remodeling the space. But I secretly hoped she didn't change a thing. Of all the rooms in the house, the kitchen was where my childhood nostalgia was most firmly rooted, and I wasn't ready to let go of that quite yet.

After filling Hudson in on what had happened at Swede's earlier in the day—Norma walking off the job was almost as newsworthy as finding out Martha had been poisoned—I recounted my grandmother's confrontation with Chief Jeong.

"You should have seen it. The chief had a ten-minute rant about the Olson women meddling in police business. My grandmother was as cool as a cucumber. She smiled, nodded, and made soothing noises while Chief Jeong yelled. Then, when she ran out of steam, Grandma patted her on the arm and said, 'There, there, dear.'"

Hudson chuckled. "I wish I had been there for that."

"Wait, that's not the best part." I leaned forward, doing a dramatic drum roll on the table. Dr. McCoy was not impressed. Petting was not to be interrupted unless it was his decision. At least that's how I interpreted the cat's plaintive meowing.

After a few placating scratches behind the cat's ears, I said, "Grandma asked Chief Jeong if she had signed up for a library card since moving to town. When the chief asked why, my grandmother smiled sweetly and said there was a helpful collection of anger management books she might want to check out."

"Way to go, Rose," Hudson exclaimed.

"I've had a lot of experience dealing with irate folks in my years as a librarian. Usually, I handle this type of situation better. I'm not sure what happened." Grandma looked sheepish as she continued, "Antagonizing the chief of police wasn't a good idea.

We need her on our side if we're going to investigate Martha's death."

"I'm glad you held your own with her," I said. "Now, she knows you're not a pushover. She'll take you seriously."

"I'm not so sure about that." The kitchen timer rang, and Grandma got up from the table. "Let me check the muffins, and after we can figure out our next steps."

"What kind of muffins are you making?" Hudson asked. "They smell great."

"They're ricotta chocolate chip." My grandmother pulled the muffin tins out of the oven and set them on a rack. "The ricotta cheese keeps them moist."

I felt my eyes get teary. "Those are the muffins Martha was talking about when Hudson and I saw her earlier today."

Grandma nodded. "After you told me about that, I thought I'd make a batch in her honor."

As my grandmother was pulling off her oven mitts, Grandpa walked into the kitchen and sniffed the air. "Muffins?"

"Hands off, Thor," my grandmother warned. "They need to cool for a while. I'll let you know when they're ready to eat."

Grandpa nodded, and looked at Hudson. "Twine?"

Fortunately, Hudson was used to my grandfather's stoic nature and preference for communicating with as few words as possible. He reached into the messenger bag by his feet. "Yes, sir. I've got a bunch of good pieces here that I think you'll like."

After inspecting the scraps of twine carefully, my grandfather nodded his approval, and stuffed them into the pocket of his overalls. When he glanced back at the muffins, Grandma shooed him away. "Go out to the barn, Thor. I'll let you know when they're ready to eat."

While I filled up our coffee cups, Hudson mentioned the project my grandfather was working on. "If Thor ties anymore twine on that ball, he'll need to take off the barn doors to get it out of there."

"Oh, that ball of twine isn't going anywhere," I said. "Grandpa hopes that it'll become a tourist attraction one day, like that one in Kansas."

"He has to get into the Guinness Book of World Records first," my grandmother pointed out. "Having his ball of twine be officially declared the largest in America has been Thor's dream for years. But I'm not sure how I feel about a bunch of strangers roaming around our property, though."

"You could charge admission," I suggested. "And sell refreshments."

Grandma scoffed as she sat down at the table. "Who would pay to see a bunch of twine?"

"You'd be surprised," Hudson said. "I paid good money to go to the Bigfoot Museum once."

"How was it?" I asked.

"Really fun," he said. "This woman in the town I

used to live in organized the trip. She had planned another trip to go see a UFO exhibition. I really wanted to go on it, but I was getting ready to move to North Dakota, so I missed out. I should email Mollie and tell her about Thor's ball of twine. It's exactly the type of thing she'd love."

"Has Grandpa heard anything back from the Guinness people?" I asked.

Grandma shook her head. "Not yet. I don't think I've ever seen him more anxious about anything in my life."

"How can you tell when Thor is anxious?" Hudson asked. "I find him really hard to read."

"When you've been married as long as we have, you know how someone is feeling, even if they don't show it." My grandmother took a long sip of her coffee. "Okay, time to get down to business. I think we should walk through everything we know. Thea, why don't you start? Take us through what Audra said before you were interrupted by my little 'discussion' with Chief Jeong."

My grandmother's use of air quotes around the word 'discussion' made me laugh. The chief certainly brought out an uncharacteristic side of her. My expression turned more serious as I explained that, according to Audra, Martha had been dead for several hours when she found her. After doing some mental arithmetic, I added, "That would put her time of death not too long after Hudson and I left."

"You and Hudson left around noon, right?" my grandmother asked.

"Correct," I said. "Do you have some paper to jot this down? My notebook is upstairs, and obviously with a cat on my lap, I'm not going anywhere."

"Do you want me to take him?" Hudson offered.

I stroked Dr. McCoy. "No, that's okay. He's comfortable where he is."

Grandma pulled a scratch pad out of the junk drawer. She handed it to me, and went over to take the muffins out of the tins to continue cooling. The smell of warm chocolate was distracting me. Grandpa wasn't the only one eager to sample them.

Dr. McCoy wasn't happy that I had assumed secretarial duties and stopped paying sufficient attention to him. So, he hopped onto the table and sprawled out in front of Hudson.

"Okay, we have the approximate time of death. Sometime around, say, one o'clock. That's assuming when Audra said Martha had been dead for several hours, she meant more than two hours. But that makes the timeline quite tight," I said.

"Right," Hudson said. "The killer would have had to be at Martha's house not long after we left. Do you remember if we passed anyone on our way back into town?"

"I don't think we did. But there are a couple of other ways to get to Martha's, not just the road we took," I said. "Maybe we can get a better sense of

Martha's time of death once the coroner completes the postmortem. In any event, we know the cause of death—poison. So, if it was poison, the killer wouldn't have to be present to murder their victim."

My grandmother furrowed her brow. "Do we know it was poison for certain?"

"Leif said she had been poisoned," I pointed out. "Someone on scene must have told him that."

"But how would they know it was poison? Was there a bottle labeled 'Poison: Don't Eat or Drink' lying next to Martha's body?"

"That's a good point." Hudson took a sip of coffee before he looked at me. "It's a bit different this time around. In the past, you've been the one to find the bodies. You had firsthand knowledge. Now we have to rely on others to get information."

"We need to see photos of the crime scene," I said, shooting Leif a text. I wasn't sure if he'd come through for me, but it was worth a try.

"Talking with Audra again wouldn't be a bad idea," Hudson suggested.

I gave my grandmother a sly grin. "Agreed. Our conversation got cut short on account of a certain someone's discussion."

"Humph." Grandma sat back down and pointed at the pad of paper. "Maybe you should focus more on potential suspects than my 'discussion' with the chief," she said, doing the air quote thing again.

Hudson rubbed his chin. "Not to put too fine a

point on it, but are we certain Martha was murdered?"

"You sound like Leif," I said to him. "But it's a fair question."

My grandmother looked in my direction. "Martha told you she believed someone was trying to kill her. I think we owe it to her to investigate what happened."

"Even if the outcome of our investigation determines it as an accidental death?" I asked. "Or we could discover Martha's fears were due to either an overactive imagination or her medical condition?"

"Yes," Grandma declared. "This isn't meant as a slight on your brother—he's a dedicated law enforcement officer—but I'm not convinced the police will bring the same focus to this that we will. I'll be the first to admit that Martha was a prickly woman who could get people's backs up, but she still deserves a thorough investigation."

Hudson gave my grandmother a thumbs up. "I'm in."

"Me, too," I said. "Martha was pretty cryptic when we were discussing who might want to kill her. She did say to start with Audra, since she prepared her food." I glanced over at the muffins, my appetite fading as I considered the possibility that someone added poison to what Martha had eaten.

"Okay, maybe Audra could have done it," Hudson said. "But why? She's only been working for Martha a few weeks and she's new to the area. What possible motive could she have?"

"Not sure, but she's the only person Martha explicitly mentioned." I scrawled Audra's name down. "Martha offered two other vague pools of suspects—family members and book collectors."

"In terms of family, Martha must have been talking about her niece," Grandma said. "We know Martha and Sharon had a falling out last month. Sharon has a clear-cut motive for wanting her aunt dispatched."

"The will," Hudson and I said in unison.

My grandmother nodded. "Cutting someone out of a will is a pretty strong incentive for murder."

After drawing a star next to Sharon's name to indicate that she was our number one suspect, I asked if anyone had any ideas about who the mysterious book collector might be. "Martha owned a lot of valuable books that she refused to sell. So, there's the possibility someone wanted them badly enough to kill Martha in order to get their hands on them."

"Might be worth asking George," Grandma suggested. "He might not be a collector per se, but he's in the book business."

"The owner of the Bookish Nook?" Hudson asked.

"Uh-huh. He was the one who told me Sharon was in Bozeman." I groaned. "How could I have forgotten about that? She wasn't around when her aunt died."

"We'll need to confirm that she was out of town. But her alibi doesn't clear her as a suspect since poison is the culprit." My grandmother tapped her lip for a moment before she said, "Sharon wasn't Martha's only living relative. Hmm. I wonder …"

"Are you thinking about Teddy and Robert?" I asked.

"New guy here," Hudson reminded us. "Who are Teddy and Robert?"

"Teddy was Martha's brother. The black sheep of the family," my grandmother explained. "When he got into trouble with the law and ended up in jail, his father cut him off. Teddy died twenty or so years ago. That's when Sharon and Martha grew closer."

"Teddy had two kids—Robert and Sharon," I added.

"You might need to draw me a family tree," Hudson joked. He turned to my grandmother and continued. "But if Teddy is dead, then he can't be a suspect."

"Teddy wasn't the only black sheep in the Lund family," my grandmother said. "His son, Robert—"

"Sharon's brother," I clarified.

Grandma smiled. "That's right. Anyway, Robert also served jail time. Martha refused to have anything to do with him."

"So, you think he might be back in the picture?" Hudson asked.

"Maybe. It's worth looking into." Grandma got up from the table and placed some muffins on a plate. "Thea, can you grab the butter dish?"

The kitchen door creaked open, and my grandfather stuck his head inside. "Muffins?"

My grandmother nodded. "They're ready, Thor."

While Grandma set the plate of muffins and some napkins on the table, I got a butter knife out of the drawer.

"You aren't going to stab me with that, are you?" someone asked from behind me.

I spun around and saw Leif holding up his hands in mock surrender. The sneaky guy had managed to walk into the house without me noticing. "I might unless you tell us what you know about Martha's murder," I said, brandishing the knife.

"You know I can't do that," Leif said.

"Spill," I said, pinching his arm.

"Ow, that hurts," he said.

"Want me to do it again?"

Leif jumped back. "You know, you're not very ladylike."

When Hudson snorted, I waved the butter knife in his direction. I'm not sure I looked very menacing since he snorted again. Turning back to my brother, I pleaded, "Come on, tell us something."

"Fine." Leif let out an exasperated sigh. "Who here is familiar with the signs of arsenic poisoning?"

* * *

After Leif told us an old bottle of rat poison had been found on a counter in the kitchen, he confirmed the police's current working theory. They believed that

Martha had accidentally poured some in her coffee. The liquid in her cup had tested positive for arsenic. They were still waiting for the coroner's report, but the consensus was that arsenic poisoning was likely.

"The rat poison was right next to a bottle of liquid sweetener. She must have mixed them up," Leif said in between bites of his muffin. "The arsenic might not have killed a healthy person right away, but Martha was frail."

"Are you saying the rat poison had arsenic in it?" Hudson asked. "Wasn't that outlawed ages ago?"

"It was," Leif said. "But you can find old containers of the stuff in sheds and barns all around the country."

"But on a kitchen counter?" Hudson asked.

"Martha had all kinds of things in her kitchen. Mostly books, but lots of other junk as well," I pointed out.

Hudson looked incredulous. "Yes, but a bottle of poison? Wouldn't someone have noticed and removed it?"

"Oh, I see what you're saying. Audra prepared meals for Martha. She would have been in and out of the kitchen," I said. "A health care professional wouldn't have left rat poison there. No one would have."

I chewed on my bottom lip. Or would they? Did Audra deliberately leave the rat poison in Martha's kitchen, hoping the elderly woman put it in her coffee by mistake or worse ... did Audra come back to the house early and add the poison to Martha's cup herself? Either way, it was murder.

"What else was on the counter?" Hudson asked Leif.

Leif gave him a wry smile. "What wasn't crammed on there? There was a plastic container full of seed packets, some books, some old metal canisters, a collection of troll dolls ... you get the picture."

"I know which counter you're talking about," I said. "That's where I found the sugar cubes. But I didn't see a bottle of rat poison."

"Probably because you were so mesmerized by the troll dolls," Leif said. "Those things are creepy."

Hudson looked at me. "Audra might not have noticed the bottle either. You know what that means, don't you?"

"Yeah, that complicates things. The bottle could have been sitting on the counter for a while and no one would have realized."

"What about fingerprints on the bottle?" my grandmother asked.

"I don't know what they've found yet," Leif admitted.

"Did you get my text about wanting to see the crime scene photos?" I asked my brother.

Leif held up his hands. "Look, you know I can't show them to you. And besides, it's not a crime scene. It was an accidental poisoning."

"But you can describe the scene, can't you?" Grandma said reasonably. "You've already told us about the counter."

Knowing he was powerless to resist our grandmother, Leif explained that Martha's cup of coffee had been found on the counter next to the troll dolls. The elderly woman had been lying on the floor with her walker toppled over by her side.

"It looked like Martha took a sip of her coffee, then set it back down on the counter. When she felt the effects of the arsenic, she collapsed, knocking her walker over in the process," Leif said.

"What else did you notice?" I pressed Leif. "Did anything seem out of the ordinary?"

Leif cleared his throat. "I wasn't there for very long and I didn't get a good look at Martha's body."

"Wait a minute, what happened to her pets?" Hudson asked. "Were they in the kitchen?"

"No, they had been outside at the time Martha passed away. One of the neighbors took in the cat. The nurse is looking after the dogs for now." Leif grinned at Hudson. "Thinking of adopting them?"

When Dr. McCoy let out a low growl, Hudson said, "I think that's a hard pass. This fellow would prefer to be the only furry creature in my life."

"How about you guys?" Leif asked my grandparents. "Those Pomeranians sure are cute."

"Don't be silly," Grandma said to Leif.

"Maybe," Grandpa said a moment later, not

looking up from his muffin.

My eyes snapped in my grandfather's direction. "You want to adopt a couple of dogs?"

"Let's talk about this later, Thor," my grandmother said to him. She turned and looked at the rest of us. "Martha had cataracts, so her vision would have been affected. It is possible that she could have mixed the two bottles up," she conceded.

"Did the bottles look similar? Same shape and size?" I asked.

"Yeah, both were clear glass antique-looking bottles," Leif said.

I quickly followed up with another question. "What about a label? Was there one on the rat poison bottle?"

"Yes, there was an old label. It was hard to read the writing unless you looked closely." Leif grabbed another muffin and smeared butter on it. "But just to be clear, this wasn't murder. It was an accidental poisoning."

"Want to bet?" I said quietly.

Leif refused to wager any money, pooh-poohing my gut feeling that Martha had been murdered.

"Listen, maybe the killer wasn't there at the exact moment of Martha's death," I pointed out. "But they could have placed the bottle of rat poison on the counter next to the sweetener, knowing eventually she'd mix up the two bottles. It was just a matter of biding their time."

Grandpa's eyes glazed over while we talked about my theory. He was probably thinking about the Minnesota Twins, the weather, his giant ball of twine in the barn, or tiny dogs. I was so engrossed in our discussion about arsenic, I didn't even notice when he shuffled off to bed.

Eventually, we called it a night, but not before my grandmother doled out action items. "Hudson, why don't you talk with Audra? See what you can find out about her ... does she have any connection to Martha that we don't know about? Is there a reason why she would have wanted her dead?"

"Sure. I can go by tomorrow after work," Hudson said agreeably. "I need to return those boxes anyway. Although, I guess the books belong to her estate now."

"That's a good point," I said. "We need to find out who Martha ended up leaving her estate to. Did she actually change her will or does everything still go to Sharon?"

"Thea, why don't you see if Sharon is back in town?" my grandmother said to me. "Now that we know the killer could have left the arsenic in the house before Martha died, Sharon is still on our suspect list."

"Will do. I'll also speak with George and see if he knows of any book collectors who might have been poking around, hoping to get their hands on Martha's collection." I started to take a sip of my coffee, but it was cold. As I walked over to the sink to dump the contents, I asked, "And what are you going to do, Grandma?"

"You should make more muffins," Leif said to our grandmother. "These are great."

"I'm glad you like them, dear," Grandma said. "You get us photos of Martha's kitchen and find out about the fingerprints on the bottle, and I'll whip up another batch."

"Uh, you know I can't do that," Leif said. "Besides, like I said earlier, this was an accidental poisoning. You guys need to stop meddling. There's nothing to investigate."

"Meddling is such an ugly word," Grandma said with mock sternness. "But, as you pointed out, since the police are treating it as an accidental poisoning, then there's no reason you can't share a little information with us. If you do, I'll have more time on my hands to make muffins."

Leif squirmed in his chair, but eventually the power of moist, chocolate-laden muffins won out. "I'll see what I can do."

* * *

The next morning came way too early. I had several virtual meetings scheduled, including a couple of coaching sessions and a discussion with a new client about facilitating a company values session.

Looking presentable was the easy part, although it

did take more than my normal amount of concealer to hide the dark circles under my eyes. Artifice would probably have had a thing or two to say about the make-up products I used. She would be horrified to learn that I bought them at the drugstore and not some high-end cosmetics store.

The harder part was dredging up the mental energy to be on my A game for my meetings. I tried my best to compartmentalize. Thoughts about murder were tucked away in one part of my brain so I could focus on my clients. It wasn't easy, but I soldiered through the morning. By the time lunch rolled around, I was ready for a nap.

The problem with working at home—there was always the temptation to lie down and close your eyes. Instead, I headed down to the kitchen, grabbed a large mug of coffee and a sandwich, before I powered through a couple more hours of paperwork.

It was nearing three o'clock when I shut down my laptop. I had already checked off one of the action items my grandmother had put on my to do list, namely finding out if Sharon was back in town. A quick call to the Beauty Bucket earlier confirmed Sharon was still in Bozeman. Artifice didn't know when she would be back. I ended the call quickly when Artifice began telling me how much younger I would look if I had regular facials.

Next up was a trip to the Bookish Nook. When George's name came up the previous night, the idea had been to get some leads from him about book collectors who moonlighted as murderers in their spare time.

Now I was rethinking my line of questioning. George straddled the line between informant and suspect. Sure, he bought used books to resell in his shop. But did he also deal in first editions and other valuable books on the side? Did he covet Martha's book collection in an evil 'I need those books, and I need them now, even if it's over your dead body' kind of way? That was an unknown.

Interrogative questions—When were you last in Martha's kitchen? How familiar are you with arsenic? Were you responsible for the death of that helpless old woman?—might not be the best tack to take. That sort of thing makes people clam up.

Realizing I needed to figure out a better approach to my little chat with George, I swung by Swede's first. A cup of coffee in my hand normally always helped me think more clearly. While I was there, I figured I should grab one for Hudson as well.

When I got to the library, the kids' storytime was about to start in the Imagination Room. Since the library still needed to hire a new youth librarian, Hudson had been covering the children's programs while balancing his role as library director. It was a lot, especially when we were in the midst of a murder investigation.

I stuck my head into Hudson's office and waved the

coffee at him.

"Thanks." Hudson smiled as he grabbed the cup from me. "You know we have a coffee maker in the break room. If I didn't know better, I'd say you wanted an excuse to see me."

I felt my face grow warm. Hudson was right. I had wanted an excuse to see him. How pathetic was that? I was almost thirty. You'd think I had gotten better at the art of talking with men by now.

"The coffee from Swede's is way better," I said lamely. "And, um, I wanted to check a book out."

Hudson took the lid off his cup and blew on the hot liquid. "Is Norma back?"

"Nope. It's still self-service. Although Swede does have a 'Help Wanted' sign in the window."

"I wonder what happened between the two of them?"

"Maybe that could be the next mystery we solve," I said. "After we figure out who killed Martha."

"I'm planning on heading over to Martha's place after I'm done here to speak with Audra," Hudson said as he glanced out his office door.

My eyes followed Hudson's gaze over to the kids waiting excitedly for the program to begin. I wasn't sure the new youth librarian could live up to the bar Hudson was setting with the children's storytimes. The different voices and accents he performed for each character in the books he read aloud were impressive.

Turning back to look at me, Hudson asked, "How about you? Have you had a chance to talk with George yet?"

"Not yet," I said. "I'm working up my nerve."

"What do you have to be nervous about? You're one of the most competent women I know. You always know exactly the right thing to say." Hudson held up his coffee cup. "And you also know exactly how I like my coffee."

I laughed. "Lots of milk and sugar."

Hudson chuckled. "Okay, I gotta get going. I'll stop by tonight to catch up with you and your grandmother."

"Sounds like a plan, buddy." I went in for an awkward fist bump, ended up missing Hudson's hand and knocking his coffee cup instead. "Uh, sorry about that."

Hudson wiped down the front of his cardigan. "No worries. It was just a few drops. Now, you better go check out that book you wanted."

I really didn't need to get any more books from the library. The 'to be read' pile on my nightstand was taller than my bedside lamp at this point. But in needing to keep up the pretense, I walked over to the display of new releases.

As I was deciding between a celebrity memoir and a book on how the English language had evolved, I heard a familiar voice growl at me, "Meet me in the mystery section, lady."

Perfect. Just what I needed. Maybe someone had penned a book about how to rid yourself of snarky chameleons. If so, that would immediately go to the top of my 'to be read' stack.

"Hurry up, lady, I'm waiting," the disembodied voice declared. That was the problem with chameleons—they blend into their surroundings. Edgar could be anywhere, lying in wait to annoy me with his snark.

"I'm busy," I said in an undertone.

"Up to you. The police aren't going to look into Martha's death. Accidental poisoning requires a lot less paperwork than a murder investigation," Edgar said. "But if you're happy with the killer going free ..."

"Fine!" I huffed.

Since most patrons were attending the children's storytime program, the area housing the mystery collection was deserted. Even adults without kids enjoyed watching Hudson act out various characters as he read aloud.

As I traced my fingers across the top of Louise Penny's Chief Inspector Gamache series of books, Edgar made his appearance—complete with his trademark whooshing sound and flashing lights.

"Why do you always have to be so dramatic?" I grumbled.

"I'm doing you a favor. This town is dull, you don't have a love life, and your idea of fun is recycling glass. You can use a little pizzazz in your life." Edgar pointed at himself with his thumbs. Wait a minute, do chameleons even have thumbs? While I was pondering that, he made a little jazz hand gesture before saying, "Meet Mr. Pizzazz."

I put my hands on my hips, ready to utter a forceful retort, but I drew a blank. What do you say to a reptile who thinks he's the answer to your boring life? Not that I have a boring life, mind you.

"You keep wrinkling your brow like that and the chick at the beauty salon really will need to give you a Botox injection."

"Just cut to the chase already." I rubbed the area between my eyebrows. It seemed smooth. I was still in my twenties. Did I really need to worry about wrinkles yet?

"See that book over there?" Edgar asked, interrupting my ruminations on aging. I pulled out a copy of *A Fatal Grace* by Louis Penny. "No, not that one, dummy. The next shelf over where the authors' last names begin with 'S.' Grab the one with the pale green cover."

I pulled the book off the shelf, and gasped when I saw the title—*Strong Poison.*

Edgar rolled his eyes. "Now, who's the dramatic one?"

"It's just that Martha Lund was poisoned yesterday," I said. "It's a bit of a shock seeing this book now, that's all."

"Listen, princess, I gave you a warning yesterday

that someone was going to die," Edgar said sternly. "You should have paid attention to me."

My eyes widened. "What warning?"

"Geez, lady. You have the memory of a gnat," Edgar said. "I told you to go check out the books cataloged under 615.9, remember?"

"615.9 ..." I slowly repeated. Normally, I knew the Dewey Decimal system inside and out. But for some reason, this was eluding me. I really was exhausted, but after a moment it dawned on me. "Poisons. That has to do with poisons."

"Bingo."

"Why did you have to be so cryptic?" I wanted to throttle the little reptile. "If you had come right out and told me that Martha was going to be poisoned, maybe I could have saved her."

"Sorry, lady. That's not how things work. I don't make the rules," Edgar explained after a beat. "But if it makes you feel better, you couldn't have changed her fate. But you do have a chance to make things right. Your first step is to check out this book, read it tonight, then report back here tomorrow and we'll discuss."

"Oh, is this a book club now?" I asked, still seething. But Edgar had vanished, leaving me alone with a reading assignment and a sick feeling in my stomach. Now, more than ever, I was convinced Martha's death hadn't been accidental.

Scowling, I looked at the inside flap of *Strong*

Poison. The author, Dorothy L. Sayers, was known as one of the four Queens of Crime. She, along with Agatha Christie, Ngaio Marsh, and Margery Allingham, wrote mystery novels during the 1920s and 1930s, the Golden Age of Detective Fiction.

I really wasn't sure how a book from the last century was going to help solve a present-day murder, but it had been a while since I had read one of Sayers' books.

Realizing that I really needed to get to the Bookish Nook and catch George, I closed the book. As I was adjusting my purse on my shoulder, I overheard two people having a heated discussion. It sounded like they were in the stacks behind me.

In normal circumstances, I might have gone over and reminded them to keep their voices down. When you're raised by a librarian, the instinct to silence loud conversations is second nature. But what these two people were talking about was a conversation I wanted to listen in on.

"Why did we have to meet here?" a woman with a high-pitched voice asked. "This is the last place I want to be seen."

"I told you why already," a man said. "So, you could see if there are any other of those leather-bound books here."

"And I told *you* already," the woman said defensively. "The boxes are locked up. I can't get to them. I'm leaving before someone spots me."

The man's tone became placating. "Relax. No one is going to recognize you with that oversized hoodie you're wearing."

"I want a bigger cut," the woman said angrily. "The books are worth a fortune."

The man snorted. "How would you know what they're worth?"

"That librarian said so."

"He was just trying to impress you," the man said, his southern drawl softening the harsh tone of his voice. "If you want more money, you know what you need to do."

"How am I supposed to get into the house and get more books? She's dead."

"That's not my problem. Meet me in the usual spot tomorrow with the goods."

They had to be talking about Martha. George had a southern accent. Was that who had been demanding more books? And the woman sounded a lot like Cassidy. You couldn't mistake that squeaky, high-pitched voice.

I rushed around the stack hoping to catch them, but my purse caught on the edge of a shelving unit, causing me to tumble to the ground. By the time I got up, the man and the woman were gone.

I raced through the library, frantically looking for them, but was thwarted by a group of children and their parents marching in a mock parade with Hudson in the lead. He gave me a jaunty wave while I waited for them to pass. By the time I reached the front door and looked outside, the only thing I saw was the town's buffalo standing with his head pressed to the window, watching the kids and their antics.

CHAPTER 7
TICKETY BOO

The rest of the afternoon was a bust. I hung around the library until storytime was over, and told Hudson about the conversation I had overheard. He agreed it was possible the woman had been Cassidy. She still hadn't turned up or returned his phone calls.

The man with the southern accent must have been George. He was the mysterious book collector Martha had alluded to when I saw her the day she died. Why did Martha have to be so cryptic? If only she had come right out and given me a list of suspects' names, things would be so much easier. But murder investigations are rarely simple.

It was imperative I track down George. I hurried over to the Bookish Nook, only to find the shop was closed. It wasn't even five yet, but no amount of banging on the door got a response.

Artifice poked her head out of the Beauty Bucket next door. "Hey, hon, you're going to mess up your manicure if you keep smacking your hand against that door."

I looked at my nails. One of the advantages of leaving them unvarnished was no chipped nail polish. "Do you know where George went?" I asked the beautician.

"Haven't seen him all afternoon," Artifice said. "He's losing business by closing up early. It's his own fault, letting go of his employees like that. But if you can't afford to pay your staff, what are the alternatives? Honestly, George was never good with money. Not that you make a lot selling books, right?"

"Do you make a lot doing hair?" I asked a bit snippily. "The Beauty Bucket always seems to be deserted."

Okay, that was more than a bit snippy, but the woman irritated me.

Artifice folded her arms across her chest. "That's only because people in this town think looking frumpy is acceptable. Well, it's not. People have a duty to look their best."

Beauty as a social obligation. Hmm, that was an interesting philosophy.

"Call me if you want to take care of those roots, hon," Artifice said. "We should also talk about lowlights."

Fortunately, Hudson called, sparing me from any further suggestions about fixing the state of my hair. It was a quick update. He was at Martha's place, hoping to catch Audra, but her car was gone. When I asked if she was gone for good, Hudson admitted that he had peeked in the kitchen window, worried about the same thing. But when he saw a laptop on the table, some dirty dishes in the sink, and Martha's collection of pets snoozing on the floor, he felt reassured that she would be back.

We agreed to meet back at my grandparents' place for a quick bite to eat and a debrief. I had to run a few errands first, so by the time I walked in the door, Hudson was already sitting at the kitchen table talking to my grandfather about baseball.

"Good, you're here," Grandma said to me. "Wash up and I'll get the plates on the table."

Yet another reminder of why I was moving so slowly on finding my own place to live—delicious meals lovingly prepared by my grandmother. I was intrigued by the dish she set down in front of me. Grandpa, on the other hand, looked utterly perplexed.

"Just try it, Thor," Grandma urged. "You like chicken salad."

"I think the yellow color is throwing him," I said. "He's used to chicken salad being white."

My grandfather continued to stare at the sandwich on his plate as though willing it to turn into something he recognized.

Hudson took a big bite of his sandwich, then nodded and gave my grandmother a big thumbs up. "What's in this? It's delicious."

Grandma beamed at Hudson. "Curry powder and mango chutney. I thought I'd try something new."

"That was very daring of you." I chuckled. "Grandpa doesn't do new."

My grandmother frowned at her husband, and turned back to Hudson. "It's called 'Coronation Chicken Salad.' The recipe was created in honor of Queen Elizabeth's coronation in 1953."

"I love the idea of having a recipe created in your honor." I took a bite of my sandwich. It really was delicious. The slivered almonds gave it a nice crunch. "I wonder what my namesake recipe would be?"

"Something with kiwi fruit in it," Hudson said.

"Why kiwi fruit?" I asked.

He shrugged. "Because they're cute."

I nearly fell off my chair. Did Hudson say I was cute? Even if he did, what did he mean by that? Lots of things are cute, like the Hello Kitty stickers my cousin Freya collects, the paper plate dragons the kids made last month at the library, and those videos of celebrity interviews with puppies. Saying something—or someone—was cute doesn't signify any romantic interest, right?

My grandmother looked back and forth me and Hudson before cleared her throat. She got up from the table and returned with a jar of peanut butter and a loaf of bread. When she plonked them on the table, Grandpa nodded. He held out his plate to Hudson, wordlessly offering him the offensive chicken salad sandwich. Hudson was quick to snatch it up, having almost wolfed down the one on his plate. Then my grandfather set to making himself a tried-and-true peanut butter sandwich.

"Sorry, maybe I should have made something else," Grandma said to Hudson and me. "But it's bingo night, and this seemed like a quick, fun dinner idea."

"Nonsense," I said. "Sandwiches aren't just for lunch, especially when they're as tasty as these are."

"Do you two want to come to bingo with me?" Grandma asked.

Hudson begged off. "I need to get back to Dr. McCoy. It's well past his dinnertime."

"Just make sure you serve him something he's used to," Grandma said, looking pointedly at my grandfather. "Cats don't like it when you change their routine."

"I'll go with you," I told my grandmother. "You never know what useful gossip we might pick up."

"About the case?" Hudson joked.

"That, and maybe also what happened with Norma and Swede," I mused. "I wonder what she's up to since she quit her job."

* * *

The parking lot at St. Olaf's was more crowded than usual. "Is there a big jackpot tonight?" I asked my grandmother.

"Everyone wants to get a gander at the new assistant pastor," Grandma explained as we walked down the stairs to the basement. "Pastor Antonio is young and unmarried."

"Why did you look at me like that?"

"No reason."

"Uh-huh."

My grandmother paused outside the door to the community room where bingo was held. "Well, since you don't seem to be picking up on any of Hudson's hints, I figured you aren't interested in him. So, maybe the new pastor—"

"We are not having this conversation," I said firmly. "Come on, let's find some seats."

As we were getting settled at one of the tables towards the back of the room, Artifice walked in with another woman. She squealed when she saw me, waving madly as though we were long-lost best friends.

"Can we join you?" Artifice asked, plopping down in the chair next to mine without waiting for an answer. The hairdresser squeezed my arm as she introduced the other woman. "This is my sister, Felicity. Check out her lowlights. I was thinking we could do something similar to your hair, hon."

Felicity tossed her hair back and forth so we could admire how the darker strands made her blonde hair pop with vigor. Or at least that's how Artifice described it. It looked like box standard dishwater blonde hair to me.

The woman must have given herself whiplash showing off her locks, because she rubbed the back of her neck and asked her sister if she had any acetaminophen in her purse.

"Sure thing, hon," Artifice said. She dumped the contents of her oversized bag onto the table, knocking my grandmother's bingo daubers on the floor. "Sorry about that, hon."

Artifice slid a bottle of painkillers to her sister while I picked up the daubers. "If that doesn't work, Pete can write you a prescription for something stronger."

"Ha, ha." Felicity rolled her eyes at her sister, and washed down a couple of pills with some diet soda.

"Felicity's engaged to the medical examiner," Artifice explained to us. "His patients don't exactly need prescriptions. Get it?"

"Geez, give it a rest," Felicity said. "So, what if his patients are dead? He's still a doctor."

"You're engaged to Dr. MacGruder, dear?" my grandmother asked politely. "Congratulations."

Felicity held up her hand so we could admire her ring. "Don't mind Artifice. She's just jealous. That's why we're at bingo, to hook her up with the new pastor."

"I think you might have to stand in line," I said, looking over at the group of single women crowding around Pastor Antonio.

"I don't stand in lines waiting around for men," Artifice said. "Men wait in lines for me."

"That's a sound philosophy, dear," my grandmother said to her. "Oh, I think we're about to start."

Pastor Antonio tested the microphone while the single gals dispersed back to their tables. Once everyone settled down, he said, "We've got a real treat for you folks tonight. Allow me to introduce our new bingo caller, Norma Gottlieb."

"Well, talk about a career change," I whispered to my grandmother as the former waitress took the microphone from the pastor.

"Hmm, that is interesting," Grandma said.

As bingo night progressed, I had to admit that Norma was pretty good at calling out the balls as they came out of the spinner. All those years yelling out orders to Swede in the kitchen and her no-nonsense approach came in handy. She didn't even need the microphone to be heard. That is unless someone forgot to turn their hearing aids up.

When an older gentleman asked, "Did you say B-78?" Norma sashayed over to where he was sitting. "I said G-48. Those things inside your ears? They're not jewelry, Bob. Turn them on or get out."

Bob looked sheepish as he fussed with the settings on his hearing aids, but when Norma winked at him, all was forgiven.

"Ready, folks? Next number is B-13. Thirteen. You all know what that number is, dontcha? It's unlucky for some." Norma stared at the ball in her hand and pressed her lips together. "You wanna know who's unlucky? Swede, that's who. Wanna know why? Because he's an idiot. He let me walk out and didn't even try to stop me."

My grandmother and I exchanged glances. Pastor Antonio walked over to Norma and whispered something in her ear. She shook her head, and he retreated. After tucking a strand of red hair behind her ear, Norma drew another ball.

"O-62. Sixty-two, tickety boo," Norma called out. "All the Canadians in the room know what 'tickety boo' means, dontcha?"

A woman who had moved to Why from Winnipeg a few years ago said, "It means everything is going to be all right."

Norma gave her a brittle smile. "Except it's not, is it? Nothing is all right. I don't have my job anymore and Swede still doesn't get it."

"Pass the popcorn," Artifice said to me. "This is better than those reality shows I watch."

Pastor Antonio rushed up and placed his hand gently on Norma's shoulder. "Why don't we take a short break, everyone? Grab yourself some coffee and one of those delicious cookies the Ladies' Auxiliary made."

As the pastor escorted Norma out of the room,

Artifice grumbled, "Some girls will do anything to get attention from a guy."

"Come on, let's go touch up our makeup," Felicity suggested to her sister.

"You don't think I need lowlights, do you?" I asked my grandmother after they left.

"Nonsense. Your natural hair color is gorgeous. I know so many ladies who would kill for it." My grandmother put her hand over her mouth. "Sorry. I can't believe I put it that way. Obviously, Martha's murder is on my mind."

I smiled at her. "It's okay. I knew what you meant. We all use 'kill' and 'murder' a lot when we're joking about things. Earlier today, I told someone I'd kill for a coffee."

"Maybe it's our way of dealing with such a horrible act as taking someone's life," my grandmother said softly. "It's so hard to comprehend why anyone would kill someone. Is revenge or money really that important?"

"People kill for a lot less," I pointed out.

Grandma and I sat quietly for a few minutes, contemplating Martha's death. All around us, people chatted about everyday things—there was a sale on chicken thighs at the Little Pickle, the Garden Club was looking for volunteers for the spring planting at the community park, and the rumors were in overdrive about who was going to run for mayor in the fall.

Would they all still be so carefree if they knew a murderer was running around loose in our community?

* * *

While a cup of coffee wouldn't solve Martha's murder, it would certainly help me get through the rest of the evening. I wanted to go home, but I knew my grandmother had her heart set on playing a few more rounds of bingo. Grandma also admitted to being curious about Norma. Was she going to return and finish calling bingo?

As I headed toward the kitchen where the Ladies' Auxiliary had coffee urns and trays of cookies set up, I saw a woman who looked a lot like Sharon ahead of me—a petite woman with masses of chestnut hair cascading over her shoulders. She walked briskly down the hall, her heels clicking on the linoleum floor and her flouncy hot pink skirt swishing back and forth with each step.

Marching past the kitchen, the woman made a sharp turn to the right, toward the church offices. I hurried down the hall, hoping to catch up with her. But by the time I pushed open the glass door to the reception area, Sharon had slipped into the senior pastor's office. I skidded to a halt when I heard Pastor Rob offer Sharon his condolences. Maybe now wasn't the best time to confront Sharon and ask her if she had anything to do with her aunt's murder.

I perched on a visitor chair next to the partially ajar office door and waited. Since the magazine selection on the coffee table was limited to *Highlights* and *Outdoor Life*, I listened in on the pastor and Sharon's conversation. It was bound to be more interesting than reading an article on fishing lures or doing a word search puzzle geared at the under twelve set.

Their discussion mostly seemed concerned with making arrangements for Martha's funeral service. Sharon was insisting that it be held as quickly as possible.

"It needs to take place tomorrow," she said.

"You mean this Wednesday?" Pastor Rob asked.

"Last time I checked the calendar, tomorrow is Wednesday. Unless you know something, I don't."

"Um, yes, it is Wednesday tomorrow," the pastor said. "But—"

"Good, I'm glad we're in agreement about the days of the week," Sharon snapped. "So, let's get the body in the casket and into the ground."

My jaw dropped. Did she really just say that? Arranging a funeral wasn't like ordering a pizza that would be ready in twenty minutes or your money back. And a grieving niece should show a heck of a lot more respect than that.

I tried to picture Pastor Rob's reaction to Sharon's demands. He was an easy-going kind of guy—a useful trait given his calling—but I could imagine that even Sharon might push him over the edge.

When he responded, his tone was soothing. "I understand why you want to lay your aunt to rest as soon as possible, but we have to take into consideration that your brother works offshore on an oil rig. It's my understanding that your brother can't get here until next weekend."

"What does my brother have to do with anything?" Sharon asked, her voice steely.

"Other than you, he's your aunt's only living family," Pastor Rob said. "Don't you think he should be at the funeral?"

"My aunt cut him off decades ago," Sharon said. "In her mind, I was her only relative. So, any decisions about Aunt Martha's funeral are mine, got it?"

Pastor Rob murmured something that I couldn't hear. I inched my chair closer to the door, grateful that the carpet muffled the noise. Except I didn't need to bother. Sharon's shrill voice cut across what he was saying. "If you're not going to cooperate, I'll find someone else who will."

"It's not a matter of cooperating," the pastor said placatingly. "How about if we have a simple graveside service on Friday, then we hold a celebration of Martha's life next weekend once your brother gets into town? That will give us more time to make arrangements. I know many of Why's citizens will want to turn out to pay their respects."

"Eleven tomorrow morning," Sharon snapped. "I expect to see you at the cemetery then, and not a minute later."

"But I'm not sure the medical examiner will have released Martha's body by that time," the pastor admitted.

The horrible woman didn't even bother to respond, storming out of the office instead. She nearly collided with me as I scooched my chair back.

Sharon folded her arms across her ample chest. "What are you staring at?"

A murderer sprang to mind. Instead, I made sympathetic noises. "I was so sorry to hear about Martha. You must be devastated."

"Sure," Sharon declared in a bored tone. "Devastated."

"Um, if you want to talk about it—"

She arched an eyebrow. "Oh, are you a counselor now?"

"No, but I know what it's like to lose someone."

That seemed to catch her off guard, but after a beat she narrowed her eyes. "You're starting to develop a reputation as a nosey busybody. I'm going to tell you this one time only—stay out of my way. My aunt was old. Old people die. End of story."

Sharon spun around, then marched down the hall. As she turned the corner toward the kitchen, I unclenched my fists. Even if there wasn't any clear-cut evidence to throw Sharon in a cell, at the very least, the police should lock her up for being a jerk.

Sure, people pushed your buttons at times, causing you to snap. Edgar and Artifice came to mind. But being rude to a pastor who's trying to help? Normally, I'd be sympathetic to someone in Sharon's position. Grief is an emotional roller-coaster. One minute, you're lashing out at others, and the next, you're sobbing.

But I was convinced Sharon was still our number one suspect. Odds were good that she was responsible for her aunt's death. And if you kill someone, it isn't grief you feel. It's the fear of getting caught.

I heard someone clearing their throat. Pastor Rob was standing in the doorway to his office. His neatly pressed khaki pants, crisp button-down shirt, and brown lace-up shoes gave off a casual professional vibe, but the warmth in his brown eyes and his gentle smile reflected his pastoral vocation.

"She's just upset," the pastor said to me. "Don't take what she said to heart."

I struggled with how to respond. Not wanting to get into a whole discussion about Sharon's true character, I simply said, "Thanks."

"It's hard enough to go through a divorce, but also to lose a loved one ..." Pastor Rob shook his head.

"I heard about her husband being unfaithful," I said.

The pastor stiffened, clearly uncomfortable with talking about the personal details behind the break-up of Sharon's marriage.

"Sadly, it's all over town," I added. "You know how gossip spreads."

"I suppose you're right. It's hard to keep any secrets in Why." Pastor Rob's posture relaxed. "Sharon tried to reconcile with her husband. She even drove out to Bozeman to tell him that she was willing to give him a second chance, but he told her he was going through with the divorce."

"Do you know when she went to Bozeman?" I asked, trying to piece together a timeline. We still needed to figure out when the poison had been put on the counter in Martha's kitchen. But in the meantime, if I could figure out who was where and when that would help.

"Let's see. She left on Saturday evening." The pastor rubbed his chin. "I think that's right. She had been in the church office Friday morning to donate some items for the fundraiser next month. That's when she told me about her husband and her plan to go confront him."

"Saturday evening," I repeated. "And do you know when she came back?"

"This afternoon," Pastor Rob said. "Or at least that's what she told the church secretary when she called to make an appointment to talk about the funeral arrangements. I really couldn't say for sure."

I was tempted to pull a notebook out of my purse and jot the information down, but the pastor was already giving me a funny look.

"Is there a reason why you want to know about Sharon's trip?" he asked.

"Just nosey, I guess," I said, laughing lightly. Then I continued in what I hoped was a casual tone, "Do you know if Sharon had a chance to reconcile with Martha before she passed? Maybe she went out to the farm to visit her and make up after that awful fight they had?"

Pastor Rob sighed. "You heard about that, too?"

"It's a small town." When the pastor wasn't forthcoming, I cut to the chase. "So, do you know if Sharon saw her aunt before she left for Bozeman?"

He shook his head. "I'm afraid I don't know, but I hope she did."

I thanked Pastor Rob for his help, but before I could turn and leave, he asked, "Did you want to see me about something?"

"Um, no, I mean yes ... uh, I mean ..."

He smiled at me. "No problem. I'm here whenever you need me."

As I walked back to the community room, I thought about the funeral arrangements. Would my grandmother, Hudson, and I find evidence linking Sharon to her aunt's death? Would it prevent Sharon from attending?

CHAPTER 8
BUDDY PUNCH

Two nights later, I found myself perched on a bar stool at the Tipsy Tavern, examining the sleeve of my sweater. What was that sticky puddle of liquid I had just dragged it through? Was I going to need industrial strength laundry products to remove the brownish green stain? Were antibiotic-resistant germs seeping through the fabric into my skin?

Hudson nudged me. "Remind me again. What exactly are we doing here?"

I looked around the bar, wondering the same thing. The posters of scantily clad girls adorning the walls, the old man spitting his chewing tobacco onto the floor, the fistfight that had erupted in the corner, the foul odor emanating from the men's room—it all added up to the town's preeminent dive bar.

POISONED BY THE BOOK

Definitely a place I never thought I'd be sitting in on a Thursday night, if ever.

Yet here I was. Hoping that Bobby Jorgenson would walk through the door. After Martha died, he had made himself scarce. We were hoping that he might have seen the comings and goings at Martha's farm in the days leading up to the poor woman's demise. If there was one place Bobby Jorgenson was sure to show up at, it was the Tipsy Tavern on a Thursday night when drinks were half price until nine.

When I said as much to Hudson, he nodded. After a sip of his beer, he gave me a quizzical look. "Why do you always call him by his full name? Why not just Bobby?"

"There were a number of boys named Bobby in elementary school, so the teachers used to refer to them by their first and last names to avoid confusion. In Bobby Jorgenson's case, the teachers were usually yelling when they called his name: 'Bobby Jorgenson, stop pulling Thea's hair,' 'Bobby Jorgenson, stop shooting spitballs,' 'Bobby Jorgenson, stop standing on your desk,' and so on. You get the picture."

"He must have been a handful," Hudson said.

"You have no idea," I said. "Sometimes I call him Bobby. But you're right, I often call him Bobby Jorgenson, even when I'm just thinking about him in my head."

Hudson chuckled. "Oh, is that who you dream about at night? No wonder guys like me don't stand a chance with you."

"Guys like you?" I spluttered. "Why wouldn't you stand a chance? I mean, why wouldn't guys like you?"

I quickly gulped down my ginger ale, hoping it would keep me from continuing to utter complete nonsense. Sure, who doesn't enjoy embarrassing themselves? No one, that's who. When Hudson had compared me to a kiwi fruit the other day, saying we were both cute, I wasn't sure how to read it. Being told you're like a green fuzzy fruit is one thing. But saying something about being the type of guy who didn't stand a chance with me? Well, that's way less ambiguous.

"I'm just kidding you." Hudson grinned and gave me a buddy punch on my arm.

My stomach twisted in knots as his words sunk in. He had been joking. Well, that was one hundred percent unambiguous. Hudson wasn't interested in me at all. When I gave him a buddy punch back, he looked at me with surprise. "You're stronger than you look."

Seizing on the opportunity to change the subject, I pointed out that poison was considered a classic woman's murder weapon. "You don't need brute strength to kill someone. Have you ever read *Strong Poison*?"

"By Dorothy Sayers?" Hudson asked.

"That's the one. I started reading it for, um, a book club I'm in."

"What book club is that? I thought the library book club was reading the new Chris Bohjalian book this month."

I squirmed on my barstool. How do you explain that a snarky chameleon gave you a reading assignment and then expected you to report back the next day to discuss it? Was Edgar in a snit, because I hadn't shown up yesterday for our little book club? Probably. But I had only gotten halfway through the book.

If you had asked me a few months ago if I'd be sitting in a dive bar worrying about a talking chameleon being annoyed with me all because I didn't show up to discuss a mystery novel, I'd have thought you were nuts. Granted, if I told you I let a talking chameleon boss me around, you'd think I was crazy, too.

I sighed. I needed to make a point of popping into the library tomorrow to chat with Edgar. Because the thing is, the book he selected for me to read was incredibly relevant to our investigation into Martha's death. *Strong Poison* was about a woman who was accused of murdering her ex-lover with, you guessed it, arsenic.

"Thea, you still with us?" Hudson asked, jolting me out of my musings about Edgar's reading assignment. "Tell me about this book club of yours."

"Oh, it's a new one. Just a couple of people so far." I swiveled my barstool so that I was facing Hudson. "So, have you read *Strong Poison*?"

"I don't think so. How do you like it?"

"It's great," I said. "It's part of the Lord Peter Wimsey series and it's the first book where Harriet Vane is introduced. Lord Peter falls head over heels for Harriet, despite the fact that she's in jail for murder. But she doesn't want to have anything to do with him."

Hudson looked thoughtful. "I imagine being incarcerated would put a damper on romance."

"I love the chemistry between the two of them. They have such great banter."

"Huh. Maybe I should work on my bantering skills," Hudson said.

I felt my face grow warm. "Um, yeah, sure ..."

Hudson chuckled. "You might want to work on yours as well."

Swiveling my stool back toward the bar, I averted my gaze. "Anyway, getting back to what I was saying. Poison is a great murder weapon for someone who doesn't have a lot of strength."

"You said Sharon is petite, right?"

"If by petite, you mean short, then yes. One of my friends works out at the same gym as Sharon. According to her, Sharon is serious about strength training and packs a lot of muscle on her body. I wouldn't want to run into her in a dark alley. She could beat the living crap out of me."

"So, why do you think she poisoned her aunt?"

Hudson asked as he toyed with one of the coasters. "Why not push her down the stairs or something worse?"

I shivered, thinking about what the 'something worse' could be. I supposed poison had its advantages. The killer could keep their hands clean, so to speak.

"Because Sharon thinks she's smart," I said. "No one can prove she left the rat poison on the counter."

Hudson motioned to the bartender for another round. "Okay, and how exactly are we going to prove it? I have to be honest, Thea, we've hit a brick wall with this investigation. And Sharon's not our only suspect. Don't forget there's George and Audra to look into too. Although Audra has been avoiding me. I've driven out to the farm a couple of times and left a few messages so far."

"She hasn't called you back?"

"She left a brief voicemail saying she'd try to catch me before she left town."

"I suppose Audra has another nursing assignment." I nodded thanks to the bartender as he set a ginger ale in front of me. Noting a lipstick smudge on the rim, in a shade I didn't wear, I decided I wasn't thirsty after all. Where did the lipstick come from, anyway? Were there actually other women in this place? A quick look around the bar confirmed that I was the only female present. Goodness only knew how long it had been since this glass had seen a dishwasher.

"Besides, I don't think we should be wasting our time looking into Audra," I said. "Not with Sharon having such a clear-cut motive and a hostile attitude toward, well, toward everything."

"Yeah, you're probably right," Hudson agreed. "Sure, Martha told you to investigate her, but we both know she wasn't thinking clearly."

"Hmm ... Martha was more lucid after you left, but overall, I'd agree, she wasn't all there mentally. You know, I still haven't heard what terminal illness she was suffering from. I suppose it will come out eventually when the medical examiner releases his report." I looked sharply at Hudson. "I wonder if that's how Sharon justified it. Her aunt was dying, anyway. Why not hurry up the process?"

Hudson nodded. "And make sure she didn't get cut out of the will beforehand."

"That's another loose end. We still don't know what Martha's will actually said." I looked longingly at my ginger ale. Maybe I could sip from the other side of the glass? No, that would be gross. Turning back to Hudson, I asked, "Did Sharon really inherit the estate? Or did Martha leave it to the library, or dog rescue society, or whatever charitable organization caught her fancy?"

"You can be sure Sharon will get lawyers involved if that's the case. She'll argue that her aunt wasn't of sound mind when she changed her will," Hudson said. "Sadly, it wouldn't be that hard to prove."

"Word is that Sharon is livid that the funeral didn't take place on Wednesday." I tried to suppress a smile, but failed. Sharon didn't deserve to get her way after how she treated Pastor Rob. "My grandmother found out that Martha had left written instructions that her lawyer was in charge of the arrangements. And he's insisting on holding off on deciding anything until Sharon's brother gets into town. He wants both living relatives to be involved."

"Her brother's name is Robert, right?"

"Uh-huh. I'm impressed that you remembered. Family trees can be so complicated."

"This one looked pretty straightforward," Hudson said. "Martha had a brother—"

"Teddy," I said.

"And Teddy had two kids—Sharon and Robert. Simple." Hudson waved a hand in the air. "You should see my family tree. You need a decoder ring to make sense of it."

"Do you think your family will come out to visit you?" I asked, changing the subject.

"I wouldn't hold your breath," Hudson said. "I keep telling them how great it is here, but I think they'd rather I went back to Florida to visit."

I lifted my ginger ale toward my lips before remembering the glass was dirty. Setting it back down, I asked, "Are you sure you want to stay in North Dakota? Aren't you homesick?"

"You're not getting rid of me that easily. Are you

saying you don't want me to stick around?" Hudson gave me a shy smile, then looked down at the bar.

"Of course I want you to stay. There wouldn't be the Three Investigators without you," I said.

"Murder has a way of bringing people together. Here's to many more years of finding clues, getting confessions, and breaking alibis."

Hudson raised his glass in a mock toast, and without thinking, I clinked mine against his, then took a sip of my ginger ale. Shuddering when I realized I'd picked the wrong side of the rim, I grabbed a napkin and wiped my mouth off. Only when I started digging in my purse for some lip balm, it hit me.

"We have to get Sharon to confess," I said. "It's the simplest, most direct way to prove that she intended for her aunt to die from arsenic poisoning. She's too smart to have not wiped her fingerprints off the bottle. Unless we can find someone who saw Sharon deliberately put the arsenic bottle on the counter, it's just a theory based on intuition."

Hudson nodded. "The police do prefer facts when it comes to accusing someone of murder. But how are you going to get Sharon to confess?"

"Not sure. Maybe my grandmother will have an idea."

"Want another one?" The bartender pointed at Hudson's half-empty glass. "I'm off shift soon and I want to close out your tab before I leave."

"I'm not sure." Hudson looked at me. "Do you think Bobby is going to show? Or should we call it a night?"

"Are you talking about Bobby Jorgenson?" the bartender asked. "That dude better not show his face in here unless he has a wad of cash on him. If you don't pay your bar tab, you don't drink."

"Well, this has been a wasted evening," I muttered. "When was the last time Bobby Jorgenson had more than a few bucks in his pocket?"

"Speak of the devil!" The bartender jabbed a finger in the direction of the door. Bobby Jorgenson stood in the entryway wearing gray joggers, cowboy boots, a t-shirt, and a light denim jean jacket. "Hey, put that cigarette out. You know there's no smoking in here."

Bobby took a final drag, and tossed the butt over his shoulder onto the sidewalk. He started to walk into the bar, but turned and crushed the cigarette butt with the heel of his boot. I guess he had learned some manners since I last saw him at Martha's house.

When Bobby sidled up to the corner of the bar and asked for a Pabst Blue Ribbon, the bartender held up his hand. "You gotta settle your tab first."

"Here we go," I whispered to Hudson. "He's going to whine and beg the bartender to let him run up his tab some more."

To my surprise, Bobby pulled out a wad of cash from the pocket of his jacket, peeled off some bills, and handed them to the bartender.

After checking to make sure the money wasn't counterfeit, the bartender set a beer in front of Bobby.

"Thanks, man," Bobby said, before downing the beer in two large gulps. "Can I get another one? Actually, make it two. Wanna get 'em now while they're still half-price."

Hudson motioned for a refill, and turned to me. "I'm glad you're driving."

"Your beer is non-alcoholic," I pointed out.

"Yeah, but it still feels weird to get behind the wheel after drinking beer, even if it's not going to get me inebriated."

Bobby Jorgenson smirked at Hudson, and took off his jean jacket. "Man, anyone else think it's hot in here?"

When I saw what he was wearing underneath his jacket, I broke out into laughter. "Since when did you become a K-pop boy band fan?"

Bobby scratched his head. "Huh?"

"You're wearing a BTS t-shirt," I said. "You know, only the biggest South Korean band ever."

Bobby looked down at what he was wearing. "Oh, is that who they are? I found this in the dryer at the laundromat."

When I started humming *Butter*, Hudson smiled. "I think the bigger question is why do *you* know who BTS are?"

Not wanting to admit that I had recently become

obsessed with watching BTS music videos, I ignored Hudson and focused on Bobby. "So, where did you get all the money? You're usually broke."

"From Sharon." Bobby took a more moderate sip of his second beer. "She hired me to help get the house ready for sale."

"Do you mean Martha's house?" I asked.

"Uh-huh."

"But the will hasn't been read yet," I pointed out. "Sharon is getting a little ahead of herself."

"Huh?"

"The house might not be hers to sell."

Bobby shrugged. "As long as she pays me, I'm good."

Watching Bobby slurp down his beers was making me thirsty. I asked the bartender for some ginger ale. When he looked at the mostly full glass in front of me, I made an excuse. "This one's warm." I'm not sure why I couldn't bring myself to complain about the lipstick on the glass, but I did manage to say, "Do you mind putting it in a fresh glass?"

"Sure," the bartender said with a shrug.

"Bobby, how long were you working for Martha before she passed away?" Hudson asked.

"A couple of weeks," Bobby said. "She was a nice old gal. We used to drink coffee and shoot the breeze. She sure loved her coffee. Don't know how she stood drinking it that sweet, though."

"I like mine sweet as well," Hudson said. "Lots of

milk, too."

Bobby shook his head. "Nah, man. That's how girls drink their coffee. Straight up black is how I like mine."

Hudson didn't look bothered at all by this slight on his masculinity. "Were you working there every day?"

"Yep, pretty much," Bobby said. "Martha had a lot she wanted me to do."

"You were working in the garden, right?" Hudson said. "It's at the end of the driveway between the house and the cottage. You probably would have seen most everyone who came to visit Martha."

"Sure," Bobby said.

I took a sip from my fresh, lipstick-free glass of ginger ale before I asked Bobby who exactly he saw at Martha's house during the time he was working there.

"Well, there's that nice nurse lady, the cleaning girl, and the mailman." Bobby squeezed his eyes shut as though he were concentrating. After a minute passed, I was worried he had fallen asleep. But then his eyes snapped open. After he fortified himself with the rest of his beer, he said triumphantly, "Ray Koch was there the day Martha died."

I leaned forward. "Really? Do you know why?"

"Something about seeds is what he said to me."

"Care to expound on that?" I asked.

"Huh? Ex what?"

"She means can you tell us more about what happened," Hudson explained. "Like when did Ray show up? What exactly did he say to you? Do you know what he and Martha talked about? That kind of thing."

Bobby grinned at Hudson. "Buy me another beer and I'll tell you everything you wanna know."

Once a cold, frosty beer was in front of him, Bobby filled us in on all the details. After Hudson and I had left Martha's, Audra told Bobby she was going to head into town to run some errands. About fifteen minutes after she left, Ray pulled up in his van. He came over and chatted with Bobby about Martha's greenhouse.

"I'm surprised Ray was able to drive considering his horrific paper cut injury," I muttered under my breath.

"What's that?" Bobby asked, slurring his words slightly.

"Nothing, just thinking about what a hypochondriac Ray is," I said. "What did the two of you chat about?"

"He was interested in what seeds she had growing in those tiny pots," Bobby explained. "I told him I didn't know."

"Did Martha plant the seeds herself?" I tried to picture the frail woman making her way to the greenhouse with her walker.

"Kinda," Bobby said. "I brought the potting soil and pots into the kitchen for her. Martha had laid down some newspaper on the kitchen table, so we didn't make a mess. Then she'd pull seeds out of those little brown envelopes of hers, hand 'em to me, and I popped them into the dirt."

"What happened after that?" I asked.

"I watered them, then carried the trays out to the greenhouse."

Hudson frowned. "It's too bad she never got to see her plants grow."

"Yeah. Martha had a real green thumb. She loved gardening." I looked at Bobby. "So, what happened after Ray and you talked? Did he go into the house and see Martha?"

"Uh-huh. He wasn't there long, though. Maybe ten minutes. Came out in a hurry and sped away in his van."

Hudson and I exchanged looks. If I wasn't already convinced that Sharon was responsible for Martha's death, Ray would definitely be a person of interest.

"What about Sharon?" Hudson asked. "Did she visit her aunt that you know of?"

"Sure, she was there a couple of times when I was working," Bobby said. "The first time they had a terrible argument. Audra and I could hear it from outside the house. And the second time ... well, let's just say it was a doozy."

Hudson asked Bobby to elaborate about what happened with Sharon at the same time I asked Bobby if anyone else was there the day Martha died.

Hudson gestured to me. "Ladies first."

"Okie dokie," Bobby said before turning to me.

"Sure, someone else was there that day. Buy me a pack of cigarettes and I'll tell you."

Before Bobby could tell us about Sharon's other visit to Martha or who else had been at Martha's the day she died, the door to the Tipsy Tavern flew open. Chief Jeong and two other police officers marched in. One of the guys shooting pool dropped his cue stick on the ground and raced toward the exit at the back.

Bobby chuckled as one of the police officers chased after the guy. "I'd hate to be that fella." But his laughter died when a meaty hand clamped onto his shoulder.

"Bobby Jorgenson, I'm placing you under arrest for the murder of Martha Lund," Chief Jeong said in a crisp tone.

CHAPTER 9
FINGERPRINTS DON'T LIE

"You can't arrest Bobby Jorgenson," I cried out. "He didn't murder Martha."

I didn't have any proof that Bobby was innocent, but I knew deep down in my gut that he wasn't a killer. Sure, he might be one of the most annoying people I knew, but a murderer? No way.

Chief Jeong looked at me coolly, and proceeded to handcuff Bobby. The poor guy looked terrified, and why wouldn't he be? His past run-ins with law enforcement usually led to a few days in the county jail, fines, and community service. Misdemeanor charges were one thing. Being accused of murder was a whole other ballgame.

"Thea, you have to help me," Bobby pleaded. "I didn't kill Martha. She was like a grandmother to me."

"I know you didn't," I assured him. "Don't worry. We'll get the charges dropped."

The chief snorted. "Good luck."

I squared my shoulders. "You should be arresting Martha's niece, Sharon, not Bobby Jorgenson."

Chief Jeong barked an order at the officer standing off to the side. "Take Mr. Jorgenson to the squad car while I deal with ... *this.*"

'This' must have referred to me, because the chief wheeled around and fixed me in her gaze. "Let me make this perfectly clear. Do not interfere in things which aren't your business."

"You arresting one of my friends is *my* business," I said.

Hudson raised an eyebrow. "Friend?"

Huh, I would have never thought of Bobby Jorgenson as a friend of mine. But sometimes the enemy of your enemy is your friend, right?

To be fair, the chief of police wasn't my enemy, but she certainly wasn't my friend. She was more like an acquaintance that I didn't particularly like. The type of person you run into at the grocery store who goes out of their way to tell you that your roots need touching up, like Artifice.

Okay, so where did that leave things? An unpleasant acquaintance arresting an annoying guy I had known since I was a kid.

I rubbed my eyes. Friends, enemies, acquaintances —though it didn't really matter what category I put people in. What mattered was justice. Pinning Martha's death on Bobby Jorgenson wasn't justice. The real killer was going to get off scot free.

"Sorry, chief," Leif called out as he rushed into the bar. My brother looked completely disheveled—shirt untucked, grass stains on his pants, and twigs in his hair. "I know you told me to wait outside, but I saw a guy tear around the corner of the bar. Officer Berg yelled at me to pursue him. I was chasing the suspect when Twinkie got in the way. I tried to dodge him, but that's when I tripped over something and fell into some bushes. Unfortunately, the suspect got away."

"Oh, you poor thing. Did you get a boo-boo?" Chief Jeong said.

Oblivious to the woman's sarcasm. Leif patted down his body. "No, I think I'm okay."

The chief narrowed her eyes. "Let's start back at the beginning. Who the heck is Twinkie?"

"It's not Twinkie," I muttered. "It's Bufford."

"Twinkie," Leif shot back at me. Then he looked at the chief. "He's our buffalo."

"Your buffalo?"

"I mean the town's buffalo," Leif spluttered. "He lives here. You must have seen him before."

"I don't have time to go wildlife watching," Chief Jeong snapped. "Why did Berg tell you to chase the suspect, anyway?"

"Berg was winded. Heartburn, I think." Leif grabbed a napkin from the bar and wiped some dirt from his cheek. "He had that extra cheeseburger at lunch."

The chief clenched her fists. "Let me see if I have this right. One of my officers can't run after a suspect because of a cheeseburger and the other one got a boo-boo because of a buffalo named after a snack cake."

"If I could just clarify something," Hudson said. "We won't know the buffalo's official name until the contest closes. Twinkie is only one of the names people are voting on."

"It's going to be Bufford," I interjected. "By a landslide."

Chief Jeong looked weary. She exhaled slowly, and said, "Olson, here's what we're going to do. I'm assigning you to K-9 duty."

Leif grinned. "Really? That would be great. I love dogs."

"Great. Congratulations. You're our official dog poop officer. You're going to patrol the town and issue citations if people don't pick up after their dogs. And if you see dog poop and you can't find who left it, then you know what to do."

Leif's smile faded. "Pick it up?"

"Correct. Make sure you stock up on plastic gloves." The chief looked at my brother impassively. "Now, go find Berg and meet me back at the station."

As the chief walked out the door, Leif slumped onto one of the bar stools. He gave me a warning look. "Not a peep out of you, Thea. Okay?"

"Not even about murder?"

Leif considered this for a moment, and gave me a resigned look. "Okay, why not?"

* * *

Despite the fact that it was after eleven, my grandmother was still up when I got back from the Tipsy Tavern. Leif had come with me, hoping there were some leftovers in the fridge he could snack on before he went home.

"How was your date?" Grandma said when she saw me.

"Very funny," I said.

Grandma turned to Leif. "What happened to you, dear?"

"It's a long story." He patted his belly. "Too long to tell on an empty stomach."

"How about I heat you up some meatloaf?" She smiled fondly at my brother. Pointing at the door leading down to the basement, she said, "Go change out of that uniform. There are some clean sweats down there you can put on. Spray some stain remover on those spots, then toss it in the washer. I'll get to it tomorrow."

"Seriously?" I rolled my eyes. "He's twenty-eight years old and you're still doing his laundry for him."

"Says the girl who lives here rent free," Leif called

out as he walked down the stairs.

"Want some meatloaf, too?" my grandmother asked.

"No, I'm okay. Thanks though." I poured myself a glass of water. "I do appreciate you letting me live here. I promise to start looking for my own place."

Grandma put a plate of leftovers in the microwave. "There's no rush, dear. Your grandfather and I love having you here."

Leif was back upstairs by the time his food was heated up. As he shoveled meatloaf and mashed potatoes into his mouth, I filled our grandmother in on what had happened at the Tipsy Tavern.

"Poor Bobby Jorgenson," Grandma said. "I'll see about getting him a lawyer tomorrow."

"Based on what Leif said, they should have an easy time getting Bobby off," I said. "It's all circumstantial evidence, and the investigation has been completely botched."

Leif put his knife and fork down. "That's not what I said."

"What did you say, dear?" Grandma asked him.

"I said that there were some issues. That's all," Leif said. "Don't go misquoting me, Thea."

"Children, stop bickering," Grandma admonished us. Then she looked at Leif's empty plate. "You were hungry. Want some dessert?"

Leif grinned. "Sure."

While Grandma dished up some ice cream, I told

her about the fingerprints on the rat poison bottle. "They were Bobby's. It was easy to match them since his prints are in the system."

Grandma paused mid-scoop. "Why were Bobby's fingerprints on the bottle?"

"When Chief Jeong questioned Bobby back at the station, he told her that he was cleaning out an old shed last week when he found it," I answered.

My brother waved a finger at me. "Don't go repeating that to anyone else. When my buddy called me to tell me what's going on, it was in confidence. I only shared what he said just to get you to stop pestering me. Seriously, Thea, I feel sorry for any guy you date. You sure know how to badger a fellow."

I stuck my tongue out at Leif, and turned back to my grandmother. "Anyway, Bobby told the chief that he brought the bottle into the kitchen to ask Martha what she wanted him to do with it. Apparently, she told him to leave it on the kitchen counter and she'd deal with it later."

Grandma set the bowl of ice cream in front of Leif, and asked if anyone wanted some coffee. As she pulled a filter out of the cupboard by the coffeemaker, she said, "I remember Leif telling us that the label was nearly worn off the bottle and hard to read. Did Bobby and Martha know it was rat poison?"

"Not according to Bobby. It was just an old vintage bottle, as far as they knew. Martha liked the looks of it." I leaned forward. "But here's the thing. According to Bobby, the bottle was empty."

My grandmother furrowed her brow. "Of course it was, dear. Martha put the contents in her coffee."

"No, you don't get it," I said. "The bottle was empty when Bobby found it and gave it to Martha."

"Ah, I see," Grandma said as she sat down. "There wasn't any rat poison in it."

"Nope." I got up from the table and grabbed some mugs. "Does anyone else feel weird drinking coffee, given how Martha died?"

"A bit," my grandmother agreed.

We were all still going to drink coffee though, that was for sure. I set the steaming mugs on the table. Grandma hesitated for a moment, and took a sip.

"This is the strangest case," she mused. "A bottle of poison without any poison in it. So did someone put arsenic in it later?"

"That's where it gets weirder," I said. "The lab tested the bottle, and it was completely free of any traces of arsenic."

Grandma looked at me sharply. "Are we sure Martha actually died of arsenic poisoning?"

"Leif, want to chime in here?" I asked my brother.

He smirked. "Nah, you're doing fine."

"Go on, dear," Grandma said.

"Technically, she didn't," I said. "According to the medical examiner, Martha had a massive heart attack."

"So, this wasn't murder, after all," Grandma said slowly.

"The arsenic caused the heart attack," I explained.

"I think I need more caffeine," she said. "Because I'm not following you. There was a rat poison bottle on the kitchen counter. But the bottle was empty. They found traces of arsenic in the coffee in Martha's cup. So where did the arsenic come from? And why did the police arrest Bobby?"

"The chief thinks Bobby poured the rat poison into Martha's cup of coffee, then once she died, he rinsed the bottle out to cover his tracks."

Grandma scoffed, "But he didn't wipe his fingerprints off? Bobby isn't the brightest turnip in the turnip truck, but he's not that stupid."

"According to the chief, fingerprints don't lie," Leif said.

I nodded. "Bobby has been in trouble with the law before. He's an easy arrest. Open and shut case."

"Hmm. I don't buy it," my grandmother said. "Remember how you texted me earlier about your plan to get Sharon to confess? Time to put that into action."

"Maybe." I tilted my head. "We have another suspect now—Ray Koch. According to Bobby, he was at the house the day Martha died. And we all know those two had bad blood between them. They were ultra-competitive when it came to gardening."

"Killing someone over a green thumb? It's an

interesting theory," my grandmother mused. She looked at me. "I think it's about time you got a new hobby starting tomorrow."

"What new hobby?" I cocked my head to one side. "Please tell me it doesn't involve glitter and paint. You know how I feel about arts and crafts."

"Gardening," my grandmother said. "Tomorrow afternoon is the monthly Garden Club meeting."

"And Ray Koch is the president," I said slowly.

Grandma nodded. "It'll be the perfect opportunity for you to question him about Martha."

"Won't Ray be suspicious if Thea starts questioning him about the murder?" Leif asked.

"Ray loves to talk about anything and everything." Grandma chuckled. "All you need to do is get the conversation started, ask a few leading questions occasionally, and he'll do the rest all on his own."

"Either that or threaten him with a paper cut," I joked. "He'll spill his guts."

CHAPTER 10
OLD BOOK SMELL

When I got to the library the next afternoon, I was stunned to see Cassidy behind the front desk sorting through books. Hudson poked his head out of his office and motioned for me to join him before I could confront her. I had been planning on going to see Edgar about our little book club before attending the Garden Club meeting, but that would have to wait.

As I walked into Hudson's office, I paused for a moment. While the bones of this room still looked the same as when my grandmother had been the library director—dark paneled walls, overflowing bookshelves, and a comfortable armchair with matching ottoman—Hudson had started to add his own touches. Grandma's framed needlepoint and family pictures had been replaced with bright modern paintings, and a cat tree now stood in front of the window.

Two visitor chairs still sat in front of Hudson's desk. One had a pile of books stacked on it and the other had a cat. I knew which one was going to be easier to move. After shifting the books to the floor, I took a seat. "What the heck is Cassidy doing here? Did she return the books she stole?"

"Rather than say she 'stole' them, let's go with 'borrowed,' okay?" Hudson opened the bottom desk drawer, pulled out the books in question, and handed them to me. "Cassidy explained what happened. I'm going to chalk it up to a misunderstanding."

I examined Martha's books. They appeared to be in the same condition as when I had seen them last weekend—three first editions with leather bindings and gilded pages. As I held them up to my nose to inhale their scent, Hudson smiled.

"Bibliophiles always love the smell of old books," he said. "It reminds me of something Ray Bradbury once said. 'If a book is new, it smells great. If a book is old, it smells even better. It smells like ancient Egypt.'"

"I'd love to go to Egypt one day," I said.

"I have a cousin who's been there," Hudson said. "She was searching for some stolen treasures."

"That sounds like something you'd read in a book or saw in a movie." I handed Martha's books back to Hudson. "I'd love to hear more about her one day. But right now, I'm really curious what Cassidy's explanation was."

"Okay, but promise this will stay between the two of us," Hudson said. "Don't tell anyone, especially your brother."

"Because Leif is a police officer?" When Hudson nodded, I folded my arms across my chest. "Oh, this should be good."

"You might have noticed that Cassidy isn't exactly the type of person who normally volunteers at the library."

I thought back to the previous Friday when Cassidy had been helping with the book sale prep. While I loved the process of sorting through books, looking at the covers, leafing through the pages, and checking out the authors' bios, Cassidy seemed bored by it all. In fact, I would go so far to say that her attitude had been one of disdain for book lovers.

"So, why is she volunteering here?" As the words slipped out of my mouth, I realized the answer. "Cassidy's doing community service, isn't she?"

"She had a choice between picking up garbage, and working at the library," Hudson said. "This was the lesser of two evils."

I thought back to what Leif had told me about court-ordered community service. It was typically for people who had committed crimes such as driving under the influence, vandalism, and petty theft. When it came to Cassidy, my money was on the latter. By taking Martha's books, she had already proven herself an accomplished thief.

When I asked Hudson to confirm my suspicion, he wavered. "I don't want to violate Cassidy's privacy."

My only response was to arch an eyebrow and wait him out.

After a few moments, Hudson said, "You win, but remember—"

"Yeah, yeah, this is just between us." I made a 'my lips are sealed' motion. "Spill the beans. What did she do? Shoplifted lipstick from the drugstore? Helped herself to money from a cash register? Stole a kid's bike?"

"You couldn't be farther from the truth. Cassidy isn't some sort of common thief. In fact, some people might say what she did was justified. I'm not saying I would, but ..." Hudson held out his hands.

Now my curiosity was really piqued. Was there really anything that could be considered a justifiable crime? If you asked my brother, he would laugh at the idea. Black and white were his favorite shades of the truth. My grandmother probably saw more gray. As for me, well, I suppose it depended on the situation.

"Go on," I said.

Hudson fiddled with some die-cut stickers on his desk for a few moments, and shoved them into a drawer. "You know that new meat-packing plant?"

"Sure, the one near Williston. What about it?"

"Well, there have been some reports about safety

violations. In fact, one worker lost a hand in one of the machines."

My stomach twisted as I rubbed my fingers together reflexively. "I heard about that. How awful."

"The guy in the accident … that was Cassidy's uncle."

"Wow, I had no idea."

"Her uncle's had a hard time getting work since. Worker's compensation is helping with the medical bills, but Cassidy's family thinks the company should do more." Hudson frowned. "The company blamed him for the accident, but others disagree with that assessment. The family pressed the plant manager for additional compensation, but he refused to budge. They're trying to get a lawyer to help them with their case, but it's taking time."

"Let me guess, Cassidy took things into her own hands," I said.

"She vandalized the company's property. Spray painted all over the walls of the plant." Hudson sighed. "Something like that was never going to change their minds about compensation, but I can see what drove her to it. The frustration of seeing a loved one suffer and knowing you're helpless to do anything about it … well, it's a lot."

"Gosh, the poor girl," I said. "Her poor family. Do you know if they've set up a fundraising site? I'd like to help if I can."

Hudson gave me the details. When I pulled up the

site on my phone and saw the pictures of Cassidy's uncle and his family's reluctant plea for help, my heart sank. One horrible accident had completely changed this man's life.

After making a donation, I looked back up at Hudson. "I wish there was more I could do to help."

"You can. Be a friend to Cassidy," Hudson said simply.

I squirmed in my chair, conscious of how I had judged the younger woman. Everyone had a back story that deserved to be heard.

Dr. McCoy must have sensed my inner turmoil. He jumped into my lap and snuggled against me. As I stroked his fur, Hudson and I talked about why Cassidy had taken Martha's books.

"She heard us talking about how valuable they were," Hudson said. "She thought she could sell them on the internet and make some money to give to her uncle."

"There has to be easier ways to make money," I said, glancing down at the cat kneading my legs.

"It was opportunistic on her part," Hudson said. "I doubt she thought through the logistics. She felt remorseful, so she brought them back."

"Hey, stop that," I said to Dr. McCoy when his claws dug through my jeans. The fluffy cat looked annoyed at me. He admonished me, meowing sharply, before jumping onto the desk and knocking Hudson's pen holder over.

As I helped Hudson pick up the assorted pens and markers off the floor, our hands brushed against each other. Definitely a spark there, I had no doubt about it. Whether it was a one-sided spark, I wasn't sure. The physical touch was like a cryptic conversation. Each person was saying something, but the meaning was unclear.

Whoa, how could I have completely forgotten about that cryptic conversation I had overheard the other day? The one between a woman that sounded like Cassidy and George.

I jammed a purple highlighter in the cup before I went and peeked out the glass door separating Hudson's office from the front desk. Cassidy was still sorting through books, carefully scanning each one into the computer system before setting them on a cart.

"Is it time for the Garden Club meeting already?" Hudson asked.

"No, but it's time for a chat with Cassidy."

* * *

Cassidy looked nervous when I asked her to join us in Hudson's office. It was a marked contrast to her demeanor the last time I had seen her. Her light-hearted self-assurance was gone. In its place was a frightened girl who couldn't make eye contact with me.

"Is this about the books?" Cassidy asked quietly, averting her eyes. "I know what I did was wrong."

Yes, she had done something wrong. And, no, she hadn't. Both were true, in a way. I wanted to wrap my arms around Cassidy and tell her everything would be okay. But I shrugged off that feeling, as difficult as it was. We still needed to get to the bottom of Martha's murder, and Cassidy might hold the key.

"Have a seat," Hudson said to Cassidy.

Dr. McCoy eyed Cassidy warily from the visitor chair he was sitting on, his tail swishing back and forth. When she moved to sit next to him, he let out a low growl and leaped on top of one of the bookshelves.

Cassidy perched on the edge of the chair Dr. McCoy had vacated. Her hands gripped the armrests as though they were a source of strength.

I sat across from her, shifting my chair slightly so that we were facing each other. "I was in the library on Tuesday afternoon," I said. "I overheard a man and a woman talking. They couldn't see me, and I couldn't see them, but I could swear the woman had been you."

I recounted the details of the conversation I had heard. How the woman had said she wanted a bigger cut and she was sure the books she had taken were worth a fortune. How the man I presumed to be George had said they weren't worth as much as she thought. She had protested. And he demanded that she get more books and meet him the next day in the usual spot.

When I finished, Cassidy's shoulders slumped and tears streamed down her face. Hudson handed her a box of tissues. After she wiped her eyes and blew her nose, she told us what we wanted to know.

"You have to understand," Cassidy said. "George was blackmailing me. He told me that if I didn't do what he wanted, he'd go to the police."

Hudson furrowed his brow. "Go to the police about what? They already know you vandalized the meat packing plant."

"That's not all I did," she said softly. "I used to work at the Bookish Nook. George caught me stealing money from the cash register. I thought he was going to call the cops on me, but he told me that if I did a favor for him, then he'd forget it ever happened."

"What was the favor?" I asked.

"Steal books from Martha Lund." Cassidy dabbed her eyes, and tossed her crumpled-up tissue in the garbage can. "He gave me a list of books he wanted."

"How were you supposed to get into Martha's house to get them?" I asked.

"That was the easy part. I pretended I was making a delivery."

"Um, that doesn't sound all that easy," I pointed out. "Martha would have taken the package, said thanks, and shut the door. It's not like she would have invited you in for a cup of coffee. You wouldn't have been able to search the house."

Cassidy flashed a grin at me. "But she wasn't home. That's what made it easy. One of my friends is the receptionist at Doc Thompson's office. She told me when Martha's appointments were. All I had to do was wait until Martha and her nurse were going to be away seeing Doc. If they came home early, I would pretend that I was there doing a delivery."

Hudson frowned. "So, you broke into Martha's house?"

"Martha probably never locked her door. Lots of people, especially older folks, don't lock their doors around here," I told Hudson. Turning back to Cassidy, I asked, "That's what you were counting on, wasn't it?"

She nodded. "It seemed like a good plan. I got there, they were gone, and I walked straight into the house. Except ..."

I burst out laughing. "Except Martha's house wasn't what you expected. How could you have possibly found the books on George's list in that mess?"

"I looked everywhere," Cassidy said. "I did find a couple that he wanted in the downstairs bathroom sink. But I was running out of time, so I just grabbed a bunch of other ones that looked valuable."

Hudson got up from his desk and paced in the small office. Dr. McCoy watched from his perch on top of the bookshelves, his tail still swishing back and forth. Hudson looked up at his cat. "What's wrong, buddy?"

When Dr. McCoy growled again, Cassidy shrank back in her chair.

"Don't worry," Hudson said to her. "His bark is worse than his bite."

"Bite?" she asked, her normally squeaky voice getting even squeakier.

"No, no," Hudson said quickly. "Dr. McCoy doesn't bite. He's usually not like this. He's a real lover boy. Not sure what's wrong with him. He's probably mad that I took away the pens he was playing with earlier. Isn't that right, buddy?"

I bit back a smile. Was there anything more adorable than a grown man cooing at his cat?

After promising Dr. McCoy that he'd get him some new catnip mice on the way home, Hudson sat back at his desk.

"Can you tell us more about George's operation?" I asked Cassidy. "Was this a regular thing he did—stealing valuable books and reselling them?"

She leaned forward. "Absolutely. He's been doing it for years. He goes around estate sales, buys up books cheap, then sends them to his cousin in Bismarck who sells them in online auctions for a fortune."

"Um, that's not really stealing," I said. "That's just doing business. Sure, it might be a little scummy, not telling the people he buys books from what they're really worth. But still, it's not illegal."

Cassidy sat back in her chair, deflated.

"It sounds like stealing the books from Martha was something new for George," Hudson said. "Makes you wonder what drove him to do that."

"I bet it was his divorce," I said. "George told me that his ex-wife cleaned him out. All he was left with was the bookstore, and as we all know, bookstores aren't big moneymakers. And the gal from the hair salon told me he had to let his employees go too, because he couldn't afford to pay them."

"That's true," Cassidy said. "There was another girl who worked for George. He let her go shortly after he, um ..."

I filled in the blank. "Fired you?"

"Yeah, that," she said softly.

"So, George was in financial straits and thought he could make a fast buck with Martha's books," Hudson said.

"Makes sense," I said. "He talked about coveting her collection. He probably pinned his hopes on getting Sharon to sell it to him when Martha died."

"But when Martha didn't die quick enough to get him out of his financial hole, he ..." Hudson's voice trailed off, but his implication was clear.

Cassidy's eyes widened. "Are you saying George killed Martha for her books?"

"Do you think he's capable of murder?" I studied Cassidy intently. She was personally acquainted with a side of George that I wasn't. Her insights into the bookseller could provide a lead for our investigation that we desperately needed.

To be honest, I had been floundering. My sight had been so squarely set on Sharon that I hadn't focused on the other suspects we had originally considered—Ray, Audra, and George—like I should have.

I reminded myself to keep my emotional distance from the younger woman. Yes, her uncle had a tragic accident, and yes, she had vandalized the plant he worked at, perhaps with good reason. But she also had admitted to entering Martha's house uninvited and stealing her books. Had it really been because George had been blackmailing her? Or had she been a willing party to the theft?

As Cassidy chewed on her bottom lip, I felt my shoulders tense. Something was off here, but I wasn't sure what it was. Then Cassidy dropped a bombshell that left me reeling.

"George killed Martha, and I can prove it," Cassidy proclaimed.

CHAPTER 11
CASH OR CHECK

"What? You have proof that George killed Martha?" Somehow, I finally managed to ask once the shock of Cassidy's announcement wore off. Hudson still looked stunned. He pressed his fingers to his temples as though trying to psychically absorb what she had said.

Cassidy puffed up like the student in class who just got the right answer. "Yep. I have proof."

Hudson shook his head, then reached for his phone. "I'm calling the police."

"Hang on a minute," I said. "Let's hear what she has to say first."

Hudson unlocked his phone screen, but he didn't dial. "Fine."

I glanced at Dr. McCoy, still perched on top of the

bookshelf, and back again at Hudson. "I guess curiosity isn't just for cats." He gave me a faint smile before turning to Cassidy and giving her an encouraging nod.

"A few weeks ago, I overheard George talking with his cousin about getting rid of Martha," Cassidy said dramatically.

"Where was this?" I asked.

"It was at the bookstore." Cassidy looked down at the floor. "This was before George fired me. A customer had some questions I couldn't answer, so I went into the back to get George. But he was on his phone, and I waited in the doorway until he finished his conversation."

Hudson shoved his phone back in his pocket, calling the police apparently forgotten. "That's when you heard George say he was going to get rid of Martha?"

Cassidy nodded. "That's right."

"Well, that's hardly proof George planned to murder the woman." Hudson frowned. "George could have meant anything by 'get rid of.'"

"Hudson is right," I said. "George isn't a fool. He wouldn't casually talk about murder in front of you."

Cassidy chewed on her bottom lip. "Yeah, but he didn't know I was there. His back was to me."

"What else did George say?" Hudson asked.

"Um, he was talking about how he needed money fast. He was late on his mortgage payments. Oh, and he said something about making a deal with Sharon. If he took care of Martha, she'd give him her aunt's book collection."

"Take care of, get rid of," I repeated slowly. "Still, it's not really proof, is it? Did George say anything else? Anything more concrete?"

The woman took a deep breath, and let it out slowly. When she spoke again, it was in hushed tones. "Yes, he said killing Martha would be like doing her a favor. She was already old and sick."

"Like a mercy killing?" Hudson asked.

Cassidy snapped her head in his direction. "Exactly. That's the word he used, 'mercy killing.'"

My blood ran cold. I wrapped my arms around myself. Whether you thought assisted suicide was right or wrong, what Cassidy had overheard wasn't that. You didn't trade a woman's life, even if she was terminally ill, to get your grubby hands on a bunch of books.

While I ruminated over the injustice of it all, Hudson pressed Cassidy for more specifics.

"Did George say how he was going to kill Martha?" he asked.

Cassidy furrowed her brow. "Something about an injection, I think."

"An injection. Okay, any other details?" Hudson asked.

"No, that was it," Cassidy said. "I could tell he was ending the call, and I ran back up front before he caught me standing there."

I had regained my composure by this point, asking Cassidy why she hadn't called the police to report the conversation.

When Cassidy gave Hudson a frantic look, he said, "I already told Thea about your situation. She understands why you would be reluctant to involve the police." Hudson looked at me, "Don't you, Thea?"

"Sure," I replied slowly.

Cassidy gave me a grateful smile, before she said, "At the time, I didn't realize George was serious. I thought it was a joke of some sort. It wasn't until later that I put two and two together."

"But you're going to have to talk to the police now," I pointed out.

"I realize that," she said, her voice trembling.

"Do you want me to give you a ride to the police station?" Hudson offered. "For moral support?"

Cassidy nodded vigorously. "Yes, please."

Hudson got up from his desk. "Okay, why don't you go grab your stuff and we'll head over there now?"

"Before you go, I have a couple of other questions for Cassidy," I said. "You returned the books you took from Martha's boxes last week."

"I did," Cassidy said. "I gave them to Hudson."

"But how did you get them back from George?" I asked. "After you took them, you gave them to him, right? That was the deal. You stole the books and George would fence them through his cousin's store in Bismarck."

She gave me a wry smile. "I stole them."

"You stole stolen books." I folded my arms across my chest. "How did you do that?"

"Well, George was out of time. He wanted me to break back into Martha's house and get some more books," Cassidy explained. "Then meet him at the roller-skating rink on Wednesday night."

"That was part of the conversation I overheard at the library earlier this week," I said. "I remember him saying to meet at your usual spot."

"I didn't know there was a roller-skating rink in town." Hudson looked at me. "We should go sometime."

"Um, sure." I glanced at Hudson, wondering if he was asking me out on a date while we were interviewing Cassidy about Martha's death and George's bookish criminal endeavors. Turning back to Cassidy, I said, "Okay, so you're at the roller-skating rink. Then what happened?"

"Well, George was mad because I didn't have any more books to give him. But there was no way I was going to get back into Martha's house after she died. It wasn't worth the risk." Cassidy pressed her lips together. "When I told him that, he went ballistic. A couple walking by even asked me if I was okay."

"Were you worried he was going to hurt you?" Hudson asked.

"Nah," Cassidy said. "I used to do Muay Thai."

The girl had martial arts training. I was impressed. Maybe that was something I should look into. Being able to defend myself was a smart idea, especially if I kept getting involved in murder investigations and confronting killers.

"Once George cooled down, I offered to help load up his car with the boxes of books he was going to take to Bismarck," Cassidy continued. "His sciatica was acting up, so I knew he'd want a hand lifting heavy stuff. So, we went back to the Bookish Nook. George showed me which boxes to put in his van. And that's when I, um, retrieved Martha's books."

She shifted in her seat. "I felt bad about what I had done, and Hudson left me so many messages about it, so ..."

As her voice trailed off, I asked, "This was when?"

"Wednesday night," Cassidy said. "It almost didn't happen. George had been laid up since Tuesday afternoon. He didn't even open his store on Wednesday. But he texted me late that afternoon, insisting I meet him that night."

Hudson looked at Dr. McCoy, who was pacing back and forth on top of the bookshelf, and turned back to Cassidy. "Why the rush?"

"Like I already said, he needs the money. He was driving to Bismarck on Thursday to take stuff to his cousin to sell." Cassidy spread her hands out. "That's all I know. Really. Let's just go to the police station and get this over with."

"Before you go, I have one final question," I said. "How did you end up working in a bookstore? Usually, people who love books want that kind of job. And you don't strike me as a big reader. No offense."

She shrugged. "You get free coffee drinks on your shift."

"Oh, I can see the appeal," I said with a smile. "Free coffee is right up my alley."

While Cassidy went to get her stuff, Hudson and I discussed what she had told us.

"You know, something doesn't add up for me," I said to Hudson. "If George made a deal with Sharon to kill her aunt in exchange for Martha's book collection, why would he resort to having Cassidy steal a few books here and there?"

Hudson leaned back on his desk. "That's a really good point."

"And the part about George injecting Martha with something to kill her?" I rubbed my arm. "I'm no expert, but I don't think people typically inject someone with arsenic."

"That's right, the arsenic was found in Martha's coffee. It was poured in there." Hudson arched an eyebrow. "Do you think she made up the whole story?"

"You gotta wonder," I said. "Tell you what, while the police are talking with Cassidy, maybe you can try to find Leif and fill him in. Let him know about the inconsistencies in Cassidy's story. Then he can take it to the chief. It might put him on her good side."

"Okay," he said. "Maybe you should come with us?"

"Wish I could, but I have the Garden Club meeting."

"That's right. You're going to see what you can find out from Ray Koch and about what he was doing at Martha's the day she was killed."

I gave Hudson a wry smile. "Remember when this investigation seemed clear-cut? We were sure Sharon did it."

"But it's a lot more interesting now, isn't it?" Hudson grabbed his car keys from the desk before he said, "Don't forget about roller skating. When this is all over, we're gonna have to check it out."

As he walked out of his office, I said quietly, "It's a date."

* * *

Today's Garden Club meeting took place in the smaller of the two library meeting rooms, a fact that some folks found upsetting.

"We always have our meeting in the room next door. This room is too cramped," one woman grumbled. She was wearing a bright pink sweatshirt which read 'Coffee, Garden, Wine, Repeat.' From the way the woman was slurring her words, I had a feeling she was already on the wine phase of her day despite the fact that it was only three in the afternoon.

Her friend echoed her sentiment. "There isn't enough room here to set up for the seed exchange." Her pale blue sweatshirt had a similar boozy sentiment: 'Will Garden for Wine.' She seemed to be enunciating her words normally. Maybe she was this afternoon's designated driver.

Ray Koch tried to smooth things over by saying, "Ladies, ladies, calm down. I've already asked the library staff to set up another table at the back of the room for the seed exchange." Then, noticing me standing off to the side, Ray added, "See, there she is already. Thea is going to get the table organized for us."

I put a hand to my chest. "Oh, I'm not a library employee. I'm here for the meeting."

Ray beamed at me. "We're always delighted to have new members. Welcome to the group. Dues are thirty dollars a year. You can write me a check, darlin'. Cash is fine too. They both spend the same."

Great. Here I thought investigating a murder would only take time away from my day job. Now it was going to cost me my actual hard-earned money. Not that thirty dollars was a lot, but still, I wasn't that into gardening. It was more my grandmother's thing.

"We're going to start the meeting soon, y'all!" Ray proclaimed, his deep voice booming in the small room. "Grab a seat. Oh, and Thea if you wouldn't mind, could you find out what's happened to that table?"

When Ray pointed toward the door, I noticed his finger had a huge bandage wrapped around it. Part of me wondered if he was still milking his paper cut for all it was worth.

Fortunately, a moment later one of the library assistants came into the room with a folding table. While he set it up, I took a seat next to the hot pink sweatshirt lady. She flashed me a grin. "I'm looking forward to the lecture, aren't you?"

"Um, sure. What's it about?"

"Ray is going to talk about medicinal plants," the pink sweatshirt lady explained. "It's such an interesting topic, don't you think?"

Her friend furrowed her brow. "Where's Audra? I thought she would have been here."

"Audra Bordey?" I asked. "Martha Lund's nurse?"

"That's the one," the woman said. "She gave a special session last week about making wreaths out of dried flowers. Ray organized it."

The blue sweatshirt lady nodded. "It was excellent."

Before I could ask if they had gotten to know Audra well, Ray motioned for silence.

Turns out medicinal plants are not all that interesting, not in the least. But as Ray droned on about how foxglove can be used to produce digoxin, a treatment for heart conditions, it gave me a chance to mentally review where things were at with the investigation.

So far, we had five suspects: Sharon, George, Cassidy, Audra, and Ray. Some people might say six, if Bobby Jorgenson was included on the list. But not me. The man was too lazy and not smart enough to plan a murder, let alone carry it out.

Sharon's motive was the most obvious—she wanted to make sure her aunt died before changing her will and disinheriting her. Besides, she was a mean-spirited woman. Despising others and not caring what happened to them were excellent qualities to have as a murderer in my opinion. I gave Sharon extra points for that.

However, George was an interesting case. According to Cassidy, he told his cousin that he made a deal with Sharon—kill her aunt and he'd get all the books. If that was the case, Sharon got even more points since she had effectively 'hired' George to commit the murder. But I had doubts about Cassidy's story. We needed to talk to George face-to-face and really get to the bottom of things.

Cassidy hadn't been on my radar screen originally, but after finding out about her police record and her involvement with George's book stealing scheme, she was on there now. Not to mention the fact that she admitted to having snuck into Martha's house to steal books. Part of me wondered if she was trying to pin the murder on George in order to divert suspicion from herself.

Next on the list was Audra. I was tempted to mentally put an 'X' next to her name. What possible motive could she have had to kill Martha? None that I could think of. But Martha had specifically mentioned Audra's name, so we needed to do our due diligence and find out more about the nurse.

Of course, there was Ray. He was still droning on about something concerning the use of herbs in traditional medicine. The man was definitely passionate about gardening, that's for sure. But was he passionate enough about plants to kill Martha because of their competitiveness when it came to the county fair?

As if reading my mind, Ray began speaking about his gardening nemesis. "Martha Lund will be dearly missed. She was an avid gardener, the past president of the Garden Club, seventeen-time winner of the county fair, and the two-time winner of the state competition. One of her roses went on to be planted in the test gardens in Oregon too."

Knowing that Martha and Ray often engaged in bitter, public fights about who grew the best flowers, I admired the man's tact and grace when he suggested that a memorial plaque in Martha's honor be placed in Why's community garden.

"I think a donation of twenty dollars from everyone should do it," Ray said. "You can come up now and pay me. Cash or check is fine. Then we'll get started with the seed exchange."

The hot pink sweatshirt lady next to me sniggered. "Memorial plaque, hah. More like a celebration plaque."

"What do you mean?" I asked her.

"Ray has been dancing on Martha's grave ever since she passed away," she confided in me. "Did you know he was trying to get Martha disqualified from the county fair this year on the grounds that she used AI to program her irrigation system?"

"I had no idea that gardeners used artificial intelligence," I said. "But I suppose you could find it in all sorts of programs and apps these days."

The woman's friend leaned forward. "It was all made up. Ray knows that he didn't stand a chance of winning on his own merits. So, he seized on something he saw on the news about AI and twisted it around."

"If human fingers didn't set the timers, then it ain't right," the hot pink sweatshirt lady said in a pretty good imitation of Ray's southern accent.

"How serious was their rivalry? Do you think Ray would have ..." I paused, trying to figure out how to phrase my question delicately.

I'm not sure if it was the wine the hot pink sweatshirt lady had drunk earlier or if she was normally so forthright, but she cackled loudly. "You're wondering if Ray killed Martha, aren't you?"

I nodded. "After what you said about him, I am curious."

"Let's just put it this way," she said. "I wouldn't put it past him."

"Especially after that incident at the International Peace Garden," the pale blue sweatshirt woman said. "The Garden Club had an outing up there last year. Have you ever been there? The flowers are lovely."

"Um, yes, when I was a kid. We took a trip to visit friends in Winnipeg and stopped there when we crossed the border," I said. "What exactly happened?"

"Well, we had finished having lunch at the cafe," the blue sweatshirt lady said. "They make a lovely grilled cheese. It was perfectly toasted and—"

The hot pink sweatshirt lady interrupted. "She doesn't care what you had for lunch. Tell her the rest of the story."

"How do you know she doesn't care?" The woman snapped at her friend, but she smiled as she turned back to me. "Do you like grilled cheese?"

"Of course. Doesn't everyone?" I replied.

"I don't." The hot pink sweatshirt lady held up her hand. "I'm lactose intolerant."

"Now who's getting off track?" her friend huffed. "Anyway, to get back to my story. We had finished lunch, and we were strolling through the formal garden when Martha fell into one of the water features. Except she didn't exactly fall, if you know what I mean ... Ray pushed her."

The hot pink sweatshirt lady gave me a knowing look. "Ray claimed that Martha tripped and that he was trying to save her. But that's not what it looked like from where we were standing."

"Ray was fuming about losing at the county fair. You'd think he would have been used to it at that point," the other woman said.

"This was last year?" I asked.

Both ladies nodded. The hot pink sweatshirt lady patted me on my knee. "Of course, we can't prove that Ray deliberately pushed Martha into the water or that he permanently eliminated his biggest rival later. But one thing I know for sure—he's not a nice man. At least not when it comes to gardening."

They shushed up when Ray came over asking for contributions to Martha's memorial plaque. After the ladies handed Ray some money, I begged off, saying I didn't have my wallet with me.

"Checks work just as well, darlin'." Ray said.

I pretended to dig through my purse. "Sorry, I don't have my checkbook on me either."

He rocked back and forth on his heels as though considering what other form of payment he could extract from me. Apparently, he was unfamiliar with the concept of transferring money from an app on your phone. "Maybe you have some change at the bottom of your purse?"

"Ray, give it a rest," the hot pink sweatshirt lady snapped. "Let's get the seed exchange started."

"Thank you," I said once she had chased Ray away. "What's a seed exchange, anyway?"

"People bring seeds to share," she said. "Sometimes, it's a partially full seed packet from the previous year. Or, in my case, I accidentally ordered ten packets of lemon cucumber seeds online. I only have space to grow a couple of plants, so the other packets are up for grabs."

"I collect seeds from my garden," her friend added. "Martha used to do that too, remember?"

"But she didn't share all of her seeds," the hot pink sweatshirt lady pointed out. "They were almost as valuable to her as her books."

The other woman chuckled. "That used to make Ray so mad. He wanted to get his hands on those marigold seeds so badly. The ones that got her the blue ribbon prize three years in a row. He even offered to buy some from her, but she refused. Anyway, enough about Ray. Let's go grab ourselves some seeds."

I followed the two garden and wine gals up to the seed exchange table, curious to see what it was all about. Ray was holding court at one end, sharing tips and tricks about the optimal temperature for germinating peas. My eyes began glazing over. As much as I enjoyed helping my grandmother out in her garden, I'd never achieve the same level of passion for plants that these folks had.

As Ray dug through a plastic bag full of his seed

packets, I noticed one that stood out—an old brown envelope with ornate writing on the front. It looked a lot like the envelopes that Martha had tucked away in her 'secret recipes' box.

When I inched forward to get a closer look, Ray mistook my interest. "Did you want to try growing some peas this year, Thea?"

"Actually, I was curious about those seeds." I pointed at the brown envelope. "Did Martha give that to you?"

Ray grabbed the seed packet out of his plastic bag and attempted to shove it in his pocket. But with his bandaged finger, he couldn't get a firm grip, and it fluttered to the ground.

We both dove to the floor at the same time, scrambling to get the envelope. Ray's plastic bag tumbled out of his hands, scattering seed packets and their contents everywhere. The other Garden Club members scrambled to sort through the seeds, yelling at each other to watch where they were stepping. In the chaos, I lost sight of the brown envelope.

When I finally got to my feet, Ray gave me an innocent look, his hands jammed in his pockets. "You were at Martha's house the day she died, weren't you? You stole those seeds from her, didn't you? Did you kill her for them?"

A hush descended over the room as everyone waited to hear the man's response.

"Who told you I was at Martha's house?" Ray

asked, focusing on my first question.

"Bobby Jorgenson saw you," I replied.

Ray laughed. "You mean the same Bobby Jorgenson who is sitting in jail right now, accused of murdering Martha? You actually believe what he says?" Then he took a step toward me, lowering his voice so that only I could hear. "I don't really think you're Garden Club material, after all. If you know what's good for you, Thea, you'll stay out of my business. Otherwise, I'll give you more than a black thumb."

CHAPTER 12
MAPLE BROWN SUGAR VS. LEMON GOJI BERRY

I wasn't going to get anything more out of Ray, especially not with everyone else in the Garden Club staring at us. There wasn't any way to pretend that my very direct line of questioning had been a joke. How do you take back asking someone if they had killed an old, sick lady for some seeds? You can't, really. So, I did something I regretted. I threw Bobby Jorgenson under the bus.

"You're right," I said lightly to Ray. "Bobby Jorgenson isn't the most reliable witness. I don't know what I was thinking."

Ray smiled at me, but it was one of those smiles that didn't quite reach his eyes. "You wouldn't be the first silly girl who was taken in by Bobby, would you, darlin'?"

I wanted to wipe that smile off Ray's face. Silly girl? I don't think so. I smiled back at Ray—an equally fake smile. I was onto him. That seed packet definitely came from Martha's secret recipe box, and she didn't give it to him willingly. Ray had moved up in the rankings, now nearly tied with Sharon on my list of suspects. It's amazing how many extra points you get on my investigation scorecard if you're a jerk.

As I turned to leave the meeting room, the pale blue sweatshirt lady pressed a packet of lemon cucumber seeds in my hand. "Don't forget what we said about the incident at the Peace Garden," she said quietly.

My nerves were frazzled after the ugly encounter with Ray. I needed a soothing cup of coffee before I tracked down Edgar, so I headed to the staff break room. Although I didn't work at the library, my volunteer work entitled me to drinks and snacks that were kept on hand. Fortunately, someone had already brewed a pot of coffee. I poured some into a mug, added a generous splash of cream, and decided to treat myself to one of the granola bars.

I was deciding between maple brown sugar and its more exotic cousin, lemon goji berry, when

Edgar appeared on top of the fridge.

"Where've you been, lady?" he demanded. "It's Friday. You were supposed to be back here two days ago for our book club meeting."

"I'm sorry." I ripped open the lemon goji berry granola bar, tore off a chunk, and placed it on a paper towel. As I set it on top of the fridge next to Edgar, I told him how crazy things had been lately. "There's been so much going on with the murder investigation. Bobby Jorgenson was arrested yesterday for Martha's murder. My grandmother got him a lawyer. Hopefully, he'll be able to get out on bail. But I'm worried that the police will pin the murder on him, and he'll get locked up for a long, long time."

"You think I don't know what's going on?" Edgar said. "If you had come back for book club on Wednesday, like I asked, then I could have helped you."

I leaned back against the counter and took a sip of my coffee while I watched Edgar nibble at the piece of granola bar. Two things struck me as odd about this conversation. One, I was defending Bobby Jorgenson, and two, I was chatting away to Edgar as though he was one of my best friends. What had happened to all the usual feelings of antagonism I had for both Bobby Jorgenson and Edgar?

"How's the granola bar?" I asked the chameleon.

"I like the maple brown sugar one better," he said, flicking his tongue back and forth to scoop up the remaining crumbs on the paper towel.

"Me, too."

Edgar swiveled his eyes around and fixed me in his gaze. "Then why the lemon goji berry?"

I shrugged. "I thought you might like it. Don't reptiles eat berries?"

"This reptile eats hotdogs," Edgar said. "It's been so long since you brought me one, I'm practically wasting away."

I finished the rest of my coffee and set my cup in the dishwasher. I sat down at the small kitchen table and motioned for Edgar to join me. One second, he was on top of the fridge, and the next he was sitting next to the salt and pepper shakers in front of me.

"How do you do that whole vanishing and reappearing trick?" I asked.

"It's called magic, lady."

When I pressed him to give me a more thorough explanation, he sighed. "Listen, lady, let's just chalk it up to one of the universe's great mysteries. We have more pressing things to talk about. Like books."

I held up my hands. "Okay ... okay. I started reading *Strong Poison,* but I haven't finished it yet."

"Were the words too big, princess? Should I have given you an easier book to read? Maybe something like *Dick and Jane Solve a Murder*?"

I narrowed my eyes. "I liked it better when you weren't being sarcastic. And besides, that's not a real book."

"How do you know?" he snapped. "Do you know every book that's ever been written?"

"Of course not," I said. "But no one is going to write a book for kids about murder."

"Remember *Hansel and Gretel*, dummy? The old witch cooks and eats kids. Can't get more gruesome than that."

"True." I grimaced. "A lot of fairy tales are pretty horrific, actually."

"Okay, moving on. Here's what you need to do." Edgar inched forward. "Get a hold of the medical examiner's report and find out what arsenic tests they ran. They haven't buried Martha yet, have they?"

"Um, no. That's a good point though. I'm not sure what happened with Martha's funeral arrangements. I think they're still waiting for Sharon's brother to get back here."

"All my points are good," Edgar huffed. "Actually, strike that. All my points are brilliant."

I rubbed my eyes, hoping when I opened them back up, the obnoxious chameleon would be gone.

No such luck.

"Why are you still here, lady? You have work to do."

"Fine, I'm going," I snapped.

As I got up from the table, Edgar said, "One more thing."

I took a long, deep breath, and exhaled slowly. This chameleon was constantly testing the limits of my patience. "What?"

"Grab me another one of those granola bars, lady. Make it maple brown sugar this time."

* * *

Later that day, Hudson and I met my grandparents at Swede's for the tail end of the early bird special. If you loved a good deal, the early bird special was where it was at in Why. Swede served up classic North Dakota favorites such as meatloaf and mashed potatoes, knoephla soup, chicken pot pie, slush burgers, and hamburger hotdish.

Occasionally, Swede decided to try his hand at his version of fusion food. In a way, it made sense. The full name of his restaurant was Swede's Norwegian Diner, a nod to the fact that he was of half Swedish and half Norwegian descent. When Swede first opened his eating establishment, he boasted about how he had fused the cuisines of both

Nordic nations. People couldn't tell the difference.

Recently, his food combinations had become more daring. Last month he served lutefisk on top of chow mein noodles. To say it wasn't a hit was an understatement. Tonight, his experiment looked more promising—Swedish meatballs served over pasta with marinara sauce. No one had the heart to tell Swede that you could get pretty much the same dish at the Italian place down the street.

While Hudson went to the kitchen to place our order, I chatted with my grandfather about his giant ball of twine. When I asked if he had heard back from the Guinness Book of World Records yet, Grandpa frowned.

"Nope," he said.

"How long does it usually take to hear back?" I asked.

"Don't know."

"How does the process work? Do they send someone out to measure your ball of twine?"

"Depends. They review your application and let you know." My grandfather always favored one and two-word answers. It made for more efficient conversations in his estimation. So, I was surprised at this detailed reply. Well, detailed for him anyway. But I guess if you spend years tying twine together, you tend to be pretty passionate about setting a world record. And for Grandpa, stringing that many words together in one sentence showed how important this was to him.

"I'm keeping my fingers crossed for you," I said.

Grandpa nodded in response.

Hudson returned to the table balancing four early bird specials on a large tray. As he set the plates down, I joked that he should moonlight as a waiter.

"No thanks," Hudson said with a wink. "My current side gig as an investigator keeps me plenty busy."

I smiled, and turned to my grandmother. "Any word on whether Norma is ever going to return? I see the help wanted sign is still in the window."

"Remember Betty from the drugstore?" Grandma said. "She told me a couple of interesting things today—one is about Norma and the other is about Audra."

I looked up from my meatballs at the mention of Swede's former waitress and Martha's former nurse, both in the same sentence. "Don't leave us hanging. What did she say?"

"Who should I start with? Norma or Audra?"

"Norma," Hudson said quickly.

"Look at you, all interested in small town gossip," I said to him.

He grinned. "How can I not be? It's all everyone is talking about at the library."

"Even more than Martha's murder?" I asked.

"Sad, but true," he said. "But you have to remember, after Bobby Jorgenson's arrest, most folks think the case is closed."

"Hudson is right, dear," my grandmother said to me. "Norma's outburst at bingo was like our very own slice of reality TV. People want to know what's going on between her and Swede."

"Okay, so what is going on?" I asked. "What did Betty say?"

Grandma teased us by having a few bites of her meatballs and pasta before she finally filled us in. "Well, Norma came into the drugstore yesterday looking to buy a pair of reading glasses."

"That doesn't seem all that interesting," I said. "Norma is older. Makes sense that she'd need some readers."

"You didn't let me finish. She asked Betty to have the reading glasses gift wrapped and delivered to Swede."

I looked at my grandmother with interest. "That's odd."

"Here's the best part," Grandma said. "Norma attached a card to the package which read, 'Don't be an idiot. Use these so you can see what's right in front of you.'"

"What's that about?" Hudson mused as he twirled pasta in his sauce.

"Well, Swede is oblivious to the fact that Norma is in love with him," my grandmother explained.

I wiped marinara sauce off my mouth. "I think that note might be a little too cryptic for Swede. She needs to come right out and tell him."

Grandma gave me a wry smile. "Sometimes, it's hard to tell people how you feel about them."

Knowing exactly what she was implying, I gave her a warning look. I pointed out that Norma and the mail carrier were an item.

"Not anymore," Grandma clarified. "They broke up last month. I think she was seeing that fellow to make Swede jealous."

"That's a terrible idea," Hudson said. "If a girl I liked was going out with another guy, she'd be off limits no matter how I felt about her. I'd assume she didn't have any feelings for me."

"It's not a game I'd play," I said quietly.

Hudson took a long sip of his water and looked directly at me. "Good."

Feeling incredibly uncomfortable, I changed the subject. "What did Betty say about Audra?"

Before answering, my grandmother offered one of her meatballs to my grandfather. The look he gave her in return was so sweet. If you didn't know him well, you wouldn't see it, but it was plain as day to me. The man loved my grandmother.

"Betty's niece lives in Bismarck. Do you

remember Marie?" Grandma asked. "She was a few years behind you in high school."

"Uh-huh. How could I forget? She was the first girl to be on Why's football team as a field goal kicker."

"That's right," Grandma said. "Anyway, you'll never guess where she works now—at the nursing agency in Bismarck that placed Audra with Martha. Apparently, Marie was chatting with a friend from their Tucson location, and she told Marie that there were rumors about Audra and one of her terminally ill patients."

"Oh, was it one of those 'younger nurse marries her elderly patient so she can inherit his estate' deals?" I asked.

Grandma shook her head. "No, this was about how one of her terminally ill patients died. Some people at the agency think Audra was an angel of death."

"Are you talking about a mercy killing?" Hudson looked at me and frowned. "Strange that we were just talking about that earlier with Cassidy."

"What's this about Cassidy?" Grandma asked.

"We'll fill you in later," I said. "Right now, I'm more interested in hearing about Audra."

My grandmother nodded. "According to Marie's friend, some people think the man asked Audra to help in ending his life. He was in terrible pain.

Other people think she decided on her own to end his life."

"Hmm. Assisted suicide or murder?" I mused. "If it's the former, then it's a tricky ethical and moral issue. But if it's the latter, then it's something way more sinister."

"Either way, we need to find out more about Audra's past," Hudson said. "Everything we know is all third hand information right now."

"You're in luck," my grandmother said. "Marie's friend is in Bismarck this weekend visiting her parents. Betty's going to get her contact information, so that you can call her tomorrow night."

Hudson nodded. "Good. That takes care of finding out more about Audra. But we can't take our eye off our other suspects."

"You're an information specialist," I said to Hudson. "That's what you studied when you got your library degree, right? Have any ideas about how we can find out more about the others?"

"I do." Hudson leaned forward and lowered his voice like he was about to reveal something librarians are sworn to keep secret. He grinned. "It's called the internet."

My grandparents headed home while Hudson and I lingered at the table, scrolling on our phones. Since we were planning on speaking with Audra's colleague tomorrow, we decided to focus on the other suspects on our list, starting with Ray.

We didn't find anything earth shattering about Ray. The only online mentions of him had to do with the Garden Club and a lawsuit he filed against the city several years ago. Suing the city didn't go well for him. He had claimed the city caused him to develop an allergy to eggs because they mowed the grass in the town square. Only it was pointed out that there wasn't any relationship between food allergies and grass allergies. The next week, Ray was seen at Swede's enjoying a cheese omelet, his egg allergy forgotten.

While we found plenty of interesting tidbits on Cassidy's social media accounts, none of them implicated her in Martha's murder. We drew a blank with Sharon as well. But when we turned our attention to George, an idea struck me.

"What do you think about taking a road trip to Bismarck?" I passed my phone to Hudson. "I found this site for a store called the Nook of Books. It's owned by a guy with the same last name as George."

"Ah, George's cousin." Hudson smiled as he handed my phone back. "After what Cassidy said about how he fences stolen books, I'd be very interested in talking to him."

"Me, too," I said. "According to their site, the bookstore is closed tomorrow due to staffing shortages, but they're open on Sunday. We could drive to Bismarck tomorrow, meet with Audra's colleague in person tomorrow night, then pay a visit to the bookstore the next day. What do you say?"

Hudson gave me a thumbs up. "Bismarck, here we come."

* * *

Mid-morning the next day Hudson and I got ready for our road trip to Bismarck. The plan was to stay at my aunt and uncle's house overnight, so Hudson brought Dr. McCoy over to my grandparents' house. After setting up his litter box in the basement, Hudson kissed his cat on the head and told him to be a good boy while he was gone. Dr. McCoy squirmed out of Hudson's arms and rushed over to my grandmother, clearly unconcerned that his human was abandoning him.

And why would he be concerned? Grandma always had a can of tuna on hand for the fluffy cat's visits, and Grandpa liked to cuddle with Dr. McCoy while they watched Minnesota Twins baseball games together.

As I watched my grandmother place a bowl of water on the floor for Dr. McCoy, my thoughts drifted to Martha's dogs. Was Audra still taking care of them? Or had Sharon already found new homes for them?

Despite the fact that the drive from Why to Bismarck was only around four hours, my grandmother had packed a picnic basket with a thermos of coffee, enough sandwiches to feed a small army, a family-size bag of corn chips, and a container of brownies. She handed the basket to Hudson, and told me to grab some cans of pop from the fridge.

"Put them in the little cooler on the counter," she said to me. "And don't forget to thank your aunt and uncle for letting you stay with them."

Memories of my grandmother reminding me to write thank-you notes to my relatives for Christmas and birthday presents filled my mind. Most of our family still lived in North Dakota—some in Bismarck and Fargo, more in Why, Williston, and other small towns in the western part of the state. A few family members had taken off for Minnesota and more far-flung parts of the country. But we were still a tight-knit bunch.

I smiled at Grandma, and put the pop into the cooler. I knew better than to protest about the over-the-top amount of food and drink she was sending us off with. It was her way of telling me she loved me.

While Hudson took the basket and cooler out to

the car, I told my grandmother what Edgar had said about arsenic poisoning tests the previous afternoon. "He was cryptic, as usual," I said. "But I think it's worth looking into. I asked Leif about it, but the chief isn't letting him get anywhere near the investigation."

"Leave it with me, dear," my grandmother said. "There's a party at the lodge tonight. Dr. MacGruder should be there. Let me see what I can get out of him."

"I didn't realize the medical examiner belonged to the lodge," I said.

"*Everyone* belongs to the lodge," she said pointedly. "Don't you think it's time you became a Prairie Dog, too?"

"I'll think about it." I smiled at my grandmother. As I picked up my overnight bag, I remembered something important. "Hey, would you mind doing me a favor? Could you get a nacho dog from Swede's for Edgar? Leave it on top of the fridge for him."

Grandma chuckled. "Sure thing, dear. It's nice to see you and your guide are getting on better."

"I wouldn't go that far," I called back over my shoulder as I walked out the door.

The drive to Bismarck was uneventful. We chatted about our favorite books, stopped at Lake Sakakawea to have our picnic lunch, and listened to music on the remainder of our journey. For a brief moment, I thought about laying my cards on the table and asking Hudson how he felt about me. Thankfully, the impulse quickly passed. Bringing up that topic of conversation would change our friendship one way or the other. I wasn't ready to find out exactly what the nature of that change would be. Especially, not with a murder still needing to be solved.

"Turn here," I said to Hudson, once we reached North Dakota's capital city. "I want to show you something before we drop our bags off at my aunt and uncle's house and we meet Marie and Audra's colleague for dinner later."

"Why are we going to a cemetery?" Hudson asked.

"There's a really cool gravesite I want you to see," I explained as Hudson parked the car. "You were talking earlier about how you went to a Bigfoot museum. We have quirky things in North Dakota, too."

"Um, yeah," Hudson said. "There's a giant ball of twine in your grandfather's barn. If that's not quirky, I don't know what is."

I conceded his point, then led him through the cemetery to the resting place of Lenard Milo Mennes. "This guy invented those little date tags we have on our license plates."

Hudson stepped closer to inspect the headstone. "Wow, they even put a depiction of a license plate on here."

"What would you want engraved on your headstone?" I asked.

"Books and a cat, of course. How about you?"

"I don't know. Maybe a magnifying glass?"

"Your mind really is focused on the investigation, isn't it?" Hudson said to me.

I chuckled. "Guess so. Come on, let's get out of here."

After freshening up at my aunt and uncle's place, Hudson and I headed to A&B Pizza. Anytime I was in Bismarck, I made a beeline for the pizzeria. I wasn't sure what I loved more—the thin crust or the fact that they cut their pizzas into squares. I kept hoping they would open a branch in Why, but no such luck yet.

When we walked into the restaurant, I saw Marie sitting at a table in the back. She wore her light brown hair in a long braid down her back, and her blue eyes still sparkled with mischief. When it came to high school pranksters, Marie had been one of the most creative. In her senior year, she had masterminded the transformation of the teacher's parking lot into a petting zoo. I had been living in Minneapolis at the time, but the news of how the principal was less than amused to find a llama taking up residency in his parking spot had still reached me.

Marie waved us over to the table and introduced us to her friend, a petite woman who wore her dark hair in a close-cropped style. "Lucia used to work in the Bismarck office until she decided to ditch us," Marie joked.

Lucia rolled her eyes at her friend. "You're just mad because I got promoted and you didn't."

Marie stuck her tongue out at Lucia, and the two of them burst into laughter. While they regained control of themselves, Hudson and I ordered drinks and a large pepperoni pizza from the waiter.

"Sorry about that," Marie said once they stopped giggling. "We haven't seen each other in ages. I miss having this goofball around the office."

"Aw, me too, babe," Lucia said to Marie.

"Well, we'll try to make it quick so you guys can catch up," I said to them.

"Nah, don't worry about it." Marie waved a hand in the air, then her expression turned serious. "Aunt Betty said you think Audra Bordey killed Martha Lund."

"That's not entirely accurate," Hudson said. "But we do want to know more about Audra. I understand she may have been involved in the, um, suspicious death of another patient."

Lucia frowned. "'Suspicious' is a good

description. There were a lot of questions when her patient died, but charges were never filed."

"What exactly happened?" I asked.

"Audra used to make this special herbal tea for her patient," Lucia said. "It was supposed to help with nausea."

A chill went down my spine as I remembered the glass jars of dried herbs lining the counters in Audra's kitchen. "What was in the tea?"

"Audra told us it was a mix of ginger, mint, and other ingredients," Lucia said. "She swore that it was harmless, and that her patient's doctor had signed off on it."

"But you don't think it was harmless, do you?" Hudson asked Lucia.

She pursed her lips. "When a patient dies from poisoning, it makes you wonder."

"What kind of poison did he die from?" I asked.

"Digoxin," Lucia said.

Remembering Ray's lecture the previous day, I asked, "But that comes from foxglove, doesn't it?"

"That's right. It's pretty to look at, but toxic if ingested." Lucia crumpled her napkin in disgust. "They found traces of it in the poor man's tea. Audra swears she didn't prepare it for him. She even had an alibi for the time when he would have drunk it. But you have to ask, how did the guy get a hold of the foxglove leaves? Did he really put it into his tea himself?"

I looked at Hudson. "Did you ever go inside the Sunflower Cottage where Audra has been staying? There was this gorgeous wreath of dried flowers over the mantel. She told me she made it herself."

Lucia tossed her mangled napkin on the table and leaned forward. "Audra knows a lot about dried flowers."

"Like foxglove?" Hudson asked slowly.

"You betcha," Lucia said. "I'm positive she ordered the dried foxglove leaves online using a fake name, then left them where the old man would 'accidentally' put them in his tea."

Marie placed her hand on Lucia's arm. "There was nothing you could do, babe."

"I could have tried harder. I could have insisted the police charge her. I could have ..." Lucia's voice trailed off as she stared blankly into space.

Marie looked at us. "Do you mind if we take off?"

"Of course not," I said.

"Come on, let's get out of here," Marie suggested to Lucia. "We can get our pizza to go and head back to my place and watch one of those cheesy rom-com movies you love."

As the two women got up from the table, Hudson asked a final question. "How did Audra end up working for Martha Lund?"

Marie sighed. "If I had my way, she wouldn't be

working for anyone. Since there were never any charges filed, the agency kept Audra on the books. So, when Martha's niece called looking for a new nurse for her aunt, they assigned Audra."

I furrowed my brow. "I guess it was just the luck of the draw that Audra worked for Martha?"

"No, not at all," Marie said. "According to the request form, Sharon specifically asked for Audra."

CHAPTER 13
GOOD COP, BAD COP

"Well, good morning, sleepyhead," I said to Hudson the next day. "Sorry I got my cousin's room, and you got stuck with the sleeper sofa in the den. It's not the most comfortable bed."

"It was fine. I've slept on worse," he said, rubbing his lower back.

"Want a cup of coffee?"

"Please. What time is it?"

"Almost eight." I rummaged through my aunt and uncle's fridge for milk, and splashed a generous amount in Hudson's mug along with a couple heaping spoonfuls of sugar.

Hudson took a sip of his coffee. "Where are your aunt and uncle?"

"They already left for work. Sunday mornings are

one of the busiest days at their bakery." I put some sourdough bread my uncle had made yesterday in the toaster, then set the butter and jam on the breakfast bar. As I got plates out of the cupboard, I smiled to myself. This whole domestic scene felt a little weird, almost like we were playing house.

"I'm sorry I missed them," Hudson said. "I wanted to thank them for letting us stay here last night."

"Now that they're empty nesters, I think they were happy to have the company." I topped up my coffee cup and checked the toaster. "They said we can come back anytime. I think they were fascinated by the fact that we're investigating a murder."

"Your uncle made a good point about Sharon too." Hudson sat on one of the kitchen stools. "Did Sharon know about the rumors of Audra helping to end her previous patient's life? Is that why she specifically requested Audra be assigned to her aunt's care, hoping she'd do the same to Martha?"

"Right, but like my aunt said, it might not have been that nefarious. Sharon might have simply seen Audra's profile online and thought she would be a good fit." I set two plates with toast on the breakfast bar and sat on the stool next to Hudson. "It does say on Audra's profile that she provides light housekeeping, cooking, and transportation services. That would have been important for Martha's care. And she was available immediately."

"I guess the next step is to talk with Sharon."

Hudson looked thoughtful as he spread butter and jam on his toast. "Hey, did your grandmother get a chance to speak with the medical examiner at the lodge last night? Are we still in the dark about the results of Martha's autopsy?"

I nodded. "I spoke to her while you were snoozing. What Dr. MacGruder told her about arsenic poisoning is fascinating. Although, I'm not sure I understand all the medical details and terminology."

Hudson held up his coffee cup. "Well, keep it simple. I'm still waking up. The caffeine hasn't kicked in yet."

"All right. Why don't we start with a fun fact? Did you know arsenic is a heavy metal that naturally occurs in the environment? You can find traces of arsenic in all sorts of things. Rocks, soil, water, air, plants, animals—you name it, you can find arsenic in it."

"Even us?" Hudson asked.

"Yep. Here's another fun fact. A lot of common foods we eat have arsenic in them. Especially seafood. Remember that shrimp pasta dish you had a couple of weeks ago? It might have had high amounts of arsenic in it." I took a sip of my coffee while Hudson absorbed this information.

Hudson slowly set his coffee cup down, and pressed his fingertips to his face as though searching for indications that he was dying of arsenic poisoning.

"Don't worry, you're okay," I said. "The type of

arsenic found in seafood is organic. Your body doesn't absorb it. But there are other foods that can have a more toxic form in them—inorganic arsenic."

"Hmm ... organic and inorganic forms of arsenic." Hudson scratched his head. "Why do I feel like I've been transported back to chemistry class?"

"I warned you it was complicated," I said with a smile. "But you don't need to understand the science behind it. I certainly don't. What's important is that inorganic arsenic is the type that kills."

"So that's how Martha died?" Hudson asked. "She ingested inorganic arsenic?"

"Correct. You get a gold star."

"How did it happen? We know it wasn't from the rat poison bottle found in her kitchen," Hudson pointed out. "There wasn't any rat poison in it. The bottle was empty."

"That's the million-dollar question," I said. "We know arsenic was in Martha's coffee cup, but how did it get there?"

"Did Doctor MacGruder have any ideas?"

"This is where it gets complicated again. Want some more coffee before I start telling you about acute and chronic arsenic poisoning?"

Hudson pushed his cup toward me. "Please."

Once we both had fresh cups of coffee in hand, I explained how someone who had received a large dose of arsenic would show symptoms of acute arsenic poisoning right away.

"Within thirty minutes, an individual could experience nausea, abdominal pain, vomiting, and other digestive issues," I said. "It could give them chest pain, arrhythmia, or low blood pressure. Their skin could even become red and swollen."

"That's gruesome," Hudson said. "Would the person die right away?"

"Yes, they could. Although they might linger for a few days." I looked down at my toast, realizing I hadn't had any of it yet. After taking a bite, I said, "But that's not what happened to Martha. She had chronic arsenic poisoning. According to the tests they ran, the poor woman had been ingesting arsenic over a period of time."

"The bad kind of arsenic, right? What did you call that again?"

"Inorganic," I said. "It's found in contaminated water and some foods like rice. People that are exposed to it over a longer period develop serious health issues such as cancer, heart disease, liver disease, and even diabetes."

"Whoa, maybe you should have started with that," Hudson said. "If what you're saying is correct, then Martha wasn't murdered after all. She was unfortunate, that's all. The arsenic came from something she ate or drank."

"Well, that's true. She did ingest it. Remember, traces of it were in her coffee."

"Yikes. It was in her tap water, wasn't it? She

would have made her coffee with it." Hudson shuddered as he looked down at his cup.

"No, it wasn't the water. That tested negative, along with the other food found in her house."

"Then how did the arsenic get into her ..." Hudson's voice trailed off as he looked in the direction of the sugar bowl next to the coffeemaker. "Oh, I get it."

"Martha used a special sugar-free sweetener," I said. "Apparently, it was hard to get, so she didn't like to share it with visitors. That's why no one else got sick. And before you ask, the sweetener wouldn't have had arsenic in it when it was manufactured. There haven't been any other reports of other consumers using the product suffering from arsenic poisoning."

"So, someone deliberately put the arsenic into her sweetener. That means the killer would have had to have access to Martha's house."

"Or had access to the sweetener before Martha got a hold of it." I leaned forward. "I just remembered something George told me when I saw him at his bookstore on Monday. He offered me a special sugar-free sweetener for my coffee drink. I think he said it was made from rutabagas."

"Let me guess," Hudson said dryly. "It's hard to get."

I grinned. "You get another gold star."

Hudson smiled back at me, then his expression sobered. "Do we know how long the killer had been poisoning Martha?"

"Not based on the medical tests. But Martha told me she started using her new sweetener a few weeks ago. And guess what was missing from the crime scene." I did a dramatic drum roll on the counter. "The container of sweetener."

"How do you know that?" Hudson asked.

"Because after I talked to my grandmother this morning, I asked Leif to check for me. Martha kept the sweetener in a distinctive enameled metal container with a pretty yellow flower pattern on it. It said candy on it, which was Martha's idea of a little joke. No one would know that it was really sweetener inside," I said. "Leif had a look and confirmed that it was missing. Which means that the—"

Hudson's eyes lit up as he finished my sentence. "The killer was there when Martha died and took the container. They wanted to make sure there wasn't any evidence of how she had died." Then he scrunched up his eyes. "I think you might have to take away one of my gold stars because, based on all this new information, I'm not sure where this leaves us in terms of suspects."

"Let's go through it step by step together," I said. "First, the killer had to put the arsenic in the sweetener. The simplest explanation is that someone who was frequently at Martha's house over the past few weeks added the arsenic."

"Well, Audra or Sharon are the likely candidates,"

Hudson said. "Well, there's Bobby Jorgenson as well, but he didn't have a motive."

"Totally agree about Audra and Sharon," I said. "They both wanted to speed up Martha's death, albeit for different reasons. Audra as an 'angel of death,' and Sharon because she's greedy."

"Okay, but the flip side of this is that someone had to remove the container of sweetener that day," Hudson pointed out. "Sharon was out of town. So, that leaves Audra."

"Unless Audra was working on Sharon's behalf. Keep in mind what Marie and Lucia said yesterday. Sharon specifically asked for Audra when she called the nursing agency. She could have made a deal with Audra, maybe playing on her sympathies, talking about how she hated to see her aunt suffer. Audra might have agreed to poison Martha, then get rid of the evidence once she had died."

"Or Audra was acting on her own," Hudson said. "Now, that would be the simplest explanation."

"True. Let's call this 'Scenario A1'—Sharon hired Audra to kill her aunt—and 'Scenario A2'—Audra acted on her own."

"Why do I feel like there's a Scenario B coming?" Hudson asked.

"If you're lucky, we might have a Scenario C, too." When Hudson groaned, I said, "I'm kidding. Okay, Scenario B has to do with George. George had access to Martha's sweetener before it was delivered to her.

He buys it in bulk and repackages it for his customers. Putting the arsenic in Martha's batch was easy peasy. Then all he had to do is sit back and wait."

"You're basing this on what Cassidy said about Sharon getting George to kill her aunt so he could get his hands on the book collection," Hudson said. "It makes sense except for one tiny detail—George wasn't there the day Martha died. He couldn't have removed the evidence."

"But what if he *was* there?" I suggested. "The night Bobby was arrested, he started to tell us about someone else who had showed up that day. But Chief Jeong slapped the handcuffs on him before he could finish his sentence. What if that person had been George?"

"It's kind of a stretch, don't you think?" Hudson asked. "Can we find out for sure from Bobby?"

"He's still in jail. I was hoping his lawyer could ask on our behalf, but that hasn't happened yet. So, what we need to do now is press George today. If we could eliminate him, great, and we'll be down to just two suspects—Audra and Sharon."

"What about Ray?" Hudson asked. "He was there the day Martha died."

"Yeah, but that was the first time in months, maybe years, since he had been at the house. I doubt he would have had access to the sweetener when the arsenic was first added." I scowled. "I really don't like the man, but I think we can scratch him off our list."

"Fair enough. It keeps things simpler. So, what's the plan?"

"George's cousin's bookstore opens at ten and it's on the other side of town. We should probably leave here around nine-thirty."

"Sounds like we have time for a second round of breakfast," Hudson said with a grin. When I got up to go make some more, he motioned for me to sit back down. "Nope, it's my turn. More toast and coffee coming up."

While he puttered around the kitchen, I smiled to myself again. This was the kind of domestic scene I could get used to—conversation over coffee and toast. Although chatting about murder at breakfast, that I could probably do without.

* * *

Later that morning, we pulled into the parking lot of a small rundown strip mall on the outskirts of Bismarck. It was one of those places that housed stores which probably struggled to stay afloat. Did people really need a business dedicated solely to replacement plastic lids for storage containers? How many folks frequented the shop that specialized in extra narrow clown shoes?

I pointed at the far end of the strip mall. "There it is. The Nook of Books."

"Isn't that the same name as George's bookstore?"

Hudson asked. "It must be a chain."

"No, George's store is called the Bookish Nook," I reminded him. "Similar, but not quite the same."

"I wonder how similar George and his cousin are," Hudson said. "Have you met his cousin before?"

"No, George is originally from South Carolina. Or is it North Carolina? I can't remember which."

"It's pretty much the same thing, isn't it?" Hudson teased, knowing how much I hated it when people mixed up North Dakota and South Dakota.

"Very funny." I smiled in spite of myself. "Anyway, George moved to *North* Dakota about twenty years ago when he got married. I'm not sure when his cousin moved here or why."

"Maybe he came for the weather? You can't beat these sunny skies we've been having so far this spring." Hudson nosed into the parking spot closest to the bookstore and turned to me. "Ready to go find out if these guys are two sides of the same coin?"

"Meaning one is the thief, and the other is the fencer?" I grinned at Hudson. "Sure, sounds fun."

As we got out of the car, Hudson asked, "Are we doing the good cop, bad cop thing?"

"Um, okay ..." I glanced at Hudson. He was dressed in one of his trademark cardigans, paired with slim fitting khaki pants, and suede oxford shoes. The whole look screamed nerdy librarian. I have to confess, it was a look I found very attractive. But it wasn't exactly a bad cop vibe. "You go in being sweet as pie, then I'll rake him over the coals."

A smile crept across Hudson's face. "You're scary."

I grinned. "You have no idea."

A bell rang as we walked into The Nook of Books. "Be right with you," a man's voice called out from the back.

While we waited, I looked around. Unlike the homey, welcoming atmosphere of George's store, this place was a pit. Instead of the aroma of coffee brewing, there was a faint odor of mold. Instead of artful and orderly displays, books were crammed on rickety shelves. Rather than comfortable seating for customers, a tattered armchair missing one leg was leaning against the wall.

"What can I do for you?" a man asked as he walked toward us. His buzz cut, stiff posture, and neat and tidy appearance made me think that he had served in the military. But the hardness in his eyes paired with the cold and calculating expression on his face had me wondering if he had been dishonorably discharged. I felt a chill go down my spine. I wasn't sure I wanted to play bad cop anymore.

Hudson smiled. "I'm Hudson Carter and this is Thea Olson."

I shook my head. Giving out our real names was a bad idea.

Buzz cut guy ignored Hudson's outstretched hand and didn't tell us his name in return. Smart move if you're a criminal.

Hudson lowered his hand, his smile fading a fraction. "I understand you sell rare books. I was looking for a first edition of *The Secret of the Crooked Cat.*"

I inwardly smiled at Hudson mentioning one of the Three Investigators mysteries. If I remembered correctly, it had been set at an abandoned amusement park. It kind of reminded me of our plans to go to the roller-skating rink. Was it a 'casual buddy' kind of plan or a date, though? What was going on between the two of us?

Snap out of it, I told myself. What was going on was two friends trying to get to the bottom of a murder mystery. This wasn't a time to focus on the possibility of romance. I refocused my attention back on the proprietor of The Nook of Books.

"Look around." Buzz cut guy scowled in our direction. "Do you see any rare books here?"

"I figured you kept them in the back." Hudson lowered his voice. "I'm not too particular about how you got your hands on them, if you know what I mean."

The man's only response was to crack his knuckles slowly. Once his fingers were primed, he curled his hands into fists.

I grabbed Hudson's arm. "Come on, let's get out of here."

"The girl is giving you some good advice, buddy."

Hudson gulped, and slowly nodded. As we were

inching backward toward the door, George walked out of the back room. "Thea? This is a surprise," he said before shooting a glance at buzz cut guy. "Hey, knock it off, Damian. This is a friend of mine. And the guy with her runs the library in Why."

Damian unclenched his fists, but he still looked ready to attack at a moment's notice. "They're asking funny questions."

George furrowed his brow. "Like what?"

"He wanted to know about first editions." Damian jabbed a finger at Hudson. "I told him I don't sell that kind of thing."

"You have to excuse my cousin." George gave us an apologetic look. "He hasn't had any breakfast yet. Low blood sugar, you know. Makes him cranky."

"Sure, we understand," Hudson said, oozing good cop vibes. "I might have some granola bars in my car. Want me to grab one for you?"

Damian grunted something undecipherable. Fortunately, George translated. "He wants to know what kind."

"Oh, um, I think they're lemon goji berry," Hudson said, scratching his chin.

Damian did not look impressed. When he started cracking his knuckles again, I piped up. "Actually, I thought I saw a maple brown sugar one."

Damian's eyes lit up at the mention of maple brown sugar. I couldn't blame him. It was a tried-and-true flavor combination, loved by humans and chameleons alike. If you're looking for a breakfast snack food to soothe scary looking booksellers with a compulsive need to crack their knuckles, maple brown sugar was the way to go.

"Okay, one granola bar coming right up. Back in a jiff," Hudson called as he darted out the door.

While Hudson was out searching his car, George asked me why we were looking for first editions in his cousin's bookstore. I was at a loss about how to respond. Should I be doing my bad cop thing now? I deliberated for a moment and went for it.

"Let's stop playing games, okay, George?" I put my hands on my hips and squared my shoulders. "Cassidy told us all about you and your cousin's little racket. You blackmailed the poor girl into stealing books from Martha, and you brought them to Damian, so he could fence them. But a few books here and there wasn't enough for you, was it? You got greedy. So, when Sharon offered to give you all of Martha's books in exchange for killing her aunt, you agreed. You poisoned her special sweetener with arsenic, didn't you?"

Before George could respond, Hudson rushed in, clutching several granola bars in his hand. He handed them to Damian as he gave me and George a questioning look. "Everything okay here?"

George arched an eyebrow. "Sure, if you consider being accused of murder okay."

"Really, Thea?" Hudson shook his head. "You

couldn't wait until I got back?"

"Sorry," I muttered before glancing in Damian's direction. The man had already wolfed down one of the granola bars and was ripping open the second. Apparently, accusations of murder took a back seat to filling his belly. "Maybe I jumped the gun a little bit."

"What the heck is this all about, anyway, Thea?" George pressed his lips together. "I thought we were friends."

"We are." The wounded expression on George's face gave me a knot in my stomach. Being the bad cop wasn't all it was cracked up to be. "But I need to know ... did you, do it?"

George threw his hands in the air. "Kill Martha? Are you insane? Why would I do that?"

Hudson put a reassuring hand on my shoulder. He said to George, "Don't blame Thea. Martha told her that she was worried someone was trying to poison her."

"And she thought I was the one who was poisoning her?" George asked disbelievingly. "She named me?"

"Well, not exactly," I said. "But she did say that she suspected a book collector ... among other people."

"Among other people," George repeated slowly. "So, let me get this straight. She didn't say she thought I was trying to kill her. Just some mysterious book collector. And there were other suspects."

"Um, yeah," I said, looking down at the ground.

"Ask him about the conversation you overheard in

the library," Hudson prompted.

My eyes shot back to George. "That's right. I heard you talking with Cassidy about stealing Martha's books. You demanded that she break into Martha's house and get more for you."

"Oh, yeah? When did this supposed conversation take place?" George folded his arms across his chest.

"Tuesday afternoon," I said.

George frowned. "Well, it wasn't me. I closed up my shop Tuesday after lunch and spent the entire afternoon at the bank in Williston trying to refinance my house, so that I could keep my store afloat. No thanks to my ex-wife."

"Can you prove you were in Williston on Tuesday afternoon?" Hudson asked.

"I shouldn't have to prove it to you," George said.

"Well, it's either us or the police," I said coolly.

"Fine," George grumbled as he wrote down his banker's information. "Give her a call tomorrow. She'll confirm I was there all afternoon signing papers."

After tucking the paper into my purse, I turned back to George. "Okay, assuming your alibi checks out, you're off the hook for that conversation I overheard at the library. But Cassidy swears she overheard you saying that you would kill Martha."

"Cassidy is a liar," George said. "I don't know what else to tell you. I fired her after finding out that she was taking money from the cash register. I should have known better than to hire her in the first place. Martha warned me about her."

"What do you mean Martha warned you?" I asked.

"Cassidy used to clean Martha's house," George said. "The stupid girl thought she could get away with stealing valuables. Martha had a lot of stuff in that house of hers, but she could still account for every single item."

I glanced at Hudson, not sure how to respond. Right now, it was George's word against Cassidy's word. There wasn't any proof that either of them were telling the truth about the other.

As if sensing what I was thinking, George said, "If you don't believe me, you can ask Sharon. She knew about Cassidy and Martha's former nurse. They were in on it together."

"Whoa, back up a second," I said. "Martha's former nurse? Where did that come from? I thought Martha fired her, because she dog-eared pages in a book."

"Well, that didn't help either," George said. "But even Martha wouldn't fire someone for that. Stealing? That she'd fire someone for."

"So, it sounds like you and Sharon are close," Hudson said.

"Sure, the Beauty Bucket is right next door to my store. We chat all the time," George said. "When she saw I had hired Cassidy, she told me what had happened at her aunt's place. Then Martha called me and said the same thing."

"When was this?" I asked.

George narrowed his eyes. "You sure do have a lot of questions."

"A woman was murdered," I snapped, back in full force bad cop mode. "Don't you think she deserves justice? Don't you think whoever killed her should be locked up? Is that person you, George? Did you kill Martha?"

"Martha was my best customer," George said. "Do you have any idea how many books she bought from me each year? It was a lot. Without her business, I would have gone under years ago. So, you tell me, does it make sense that I would want her dead?"

"Um ... well ..." I spluttered.

Before I could come up with anything coherent to say in response, George held up his hands in mock surrender. "You talked about me wanting to get my hands on Martha's collection earlier. Guilty as charged. What book lover wouldn't want that? But kill for it? Nope, not on my life."

"I have a question, too, y'all." Damian leaned against the wall. He looked more relaxed now that he had food in his belly. "How exactly did this lady die? Did somebody shoot her? Because George is a terrible shot. He couldn't hit an elephant even if it was a foot away from him."

Apparently, Damian had missed the whole poisoning discussion earlier, probably because he had been too involved in licking any remaining crumbs from the granola bar wrappers. When I explained again that Martha had died from arsenic poisoning, Damian looked thoughtful.

"That's an awful way to go," he said. "I saw a lot of that when I worked overseas. Groundwater in a lot of places around the world is naturally contaminated with arsenic. Sometimes, people don't even realize that it's contaminated. Other times, they don't have a choice since there's no other water source. Either way, though, it kills them slowly over time."

"Damian worked for an international aid agency," George explained. "Now that he's back in the States, he thought he'd try something different. I suggested he open a bookstore. Probably bad advice."

So, he wasn't ex-military after all. I looked at Damian more closely. Maybe the hardness I saw in his eyes earlier came from too many years seeing the horrors that much of humanity experienced on a daily basis. Perhaps his aggressiveness earlier with the clenched fists and knuckle cracking really had been just low blood sugar. A lot of guys with buzz cuts, a neat and tidy appearance, and good posture weren't in the military.

It was a good lesson. As my grandmother always said, 'Don't judge a book by its cover.' Assumptions about people color how we interpret their behavior. And we're easily influenced by what others think, especially if it fits a narrative we've constructed in our heads.

I shifted my gaze to George. Was that what happened here? Martha had told me she thought a book collector might be trying to kill her. George checked that box. I overheard a man that sounded like him telling Cassidy to steal books. Another check. Artifice had gossiped about George's financial straits, which was a very good motive. Check. Cassidy had even piled on more, telling us how George would get Martha's valuable book collection in exchange for killing Martha. Check again.

Yes, George was a down-on-his-luck book fanatic. But that didn't necessarily translate into a murderer.

I realized Damian was asking me a question. "Sorry. Can you repeat that?"

"I was asking how Martha got arsenic into her system," Damian said.

"They found it in her coffee," I said. "The police originally thought Martha had accidentally poured old rat poison into her coffee. But then they arrested this guy who had been working for Martha—"

"Bobby Jorgenson," George interjected. "He's the guy I told you about, Damian."

Damian nodded. "Right, the one who you got hooked on graphic novels."

"Bobby reads ... graphic novels?" I gave George a stunned look. "He always mocks people with noses in their books."

George shrugged. "Graphic novels are a great way to get people into reading."

"An excellent point," Hudson said. "We should do a display of graphic novels at the library."

"So, what happened to this Bobby fellow?" Damian asked, bringing us back to the subject at hand.

"He's still in jail, trying to get bail money together," I said. "Honestly, I think the police realize that he didn't do it. But until they get a better suspect, they're taking the easy path."

Damian smiled and gestured to Hudson and me. "And that's where you two come in. You figured you'd point the finger at my cousin."

"Well, the sweetener that killed Martha must have come from your cousin. He told me he sold it to a few private customers," I pointed out. "I'm sure Martha was one of those customers. He could have easily put arsenic in it before giving it to her."

"Where would I even get arsenic?" George asked.

"You can get anything on the dark web," I said.

Damian nodded. "That's true. And adding poison to something? Yeah, George would be able to pull that off."

"Hey, whose side are you on?" George asked.

Before Damian could answer, I told George someone had seen him at Martha's Monday afternoon. It was a complete bluff, but until we knew for sure who Bobby had seen, it was our only shot.

"Wrong. I was at my bookstore," George said. "You know that already, Thea. You came in and we chatted."

"But that wasn't until around two," I pointed out. "You could have easily driven up to Martha's a little after noon, saw that she was dead, and grabbed the container with the tainted sweetener."

"Was I supposed to have used my magical intuition to know that she had just died and then speed up there? Um, yeah, I don't think so," George said. "I was in my shop with customers from ten that morning until I closed up. You can check my security footage if you don't believe me."

"Guess he's got you there," Damian said with a grin. "You guys aren't very good at this investigating thing, are you?"

"To be fair," Hudson said, spreading his hands out in a placating gesture. "We have lots of other suspects."

"Oh, well, that makes me feel so much better," George said, his words dripping with sarcasm.

"Who else is on your radar?" Damian asked.

"Well, there's Martha's niece, Sharon," Hudson said. "And Martha's nurse, Audra."

Damian chuckled. "So, not really lots, then?"

"Don't forget to add Cassidy to your list," George said. "She was pretty bitter about being fired by Martha."

I looked at Hudson. "If George was telling the truth about Cassidy being a cleaner at Martha's, she would have had access to the sweetener."

"Hmm ... maybe Cassidy was the person Bobby saw

that day," Hudson said.

George clapped his hands together. "Great. Are we done here? Wanna show them the door, cuz?"

As Damian ushered us out, my phone rang. "Hang on a sec. It's my grandmother."

"You'll get better reception outside," Damian said, shutting the door firmly behind us.

Actually, the reception was horrible. I had to walk to the other side of the strip mall before I could understand what my grandmother said. I looked at Hudson and mouthed, "It's Audra. She's dead."

CHAPTER 14
BIG DOGS IN TINY BODIES

"Did you really say Audra is dead?" I asked my grandmother while Hudson stared at me, his eyes wide in disbelief.

A minivan pulled into the parking lot, blaring country music, and drowning out her response. The tune was about the unexpected death of a stranger in town. It seemed appropriate for the situation. Audra had moved to Why a few weeks ago, and now, there was startling news that she was gone.

Pressing my phone close to my ear, I said, "Sorry, can you repeat that?"

"Audra killed herself, dear," my grandmother said. "She left a note saying that she couldn't live with herself after taking Martha's life."

My jaw dropped. "Audra committed suicide?"

Hudson tugged at my arm. "What's going on?" he whispered.

"Hang on a sec, Grandma." I waited to respond until Hudson and I had walked over to his car and got in, putting the speakerphone on. "Can you start at the beginning? Who told you about Audra?"

"Your brother," she explained. "You know how Chief Jeong assigned him to K-9 duty?"

"It's not really K-9 duty," I pointed out. "He hands out citations to people who don't clean up after their dogs."

"True. But he's also the police liaison to the animal shelter," Grandma explained. "Remember how Audra was looking after Martha's Pomeranians? Well, yesterday, she dropped them off at the shelter saying she couldn't care for them anymore."

"What about Sharon? Why didn't she take the poor dogs?" I asked.

"Apparently, the lady at the shelter asked the same thing," my grandmother admitted. "Audra told her that she tried to get Sharon to take them, but she refused."

Grandma paused to say something to my grandfather about putting dirty dishes in the dishwasher and not in the sink before she returned to our conversation. "Anyway, Audra said that she had a new nursing assignment and needed to leave town that afternoon to make the drive to Minnesota. She apologized for dropping the dogs off without notice.

But the assignment came through at the last minute and she was eager to get going."

Hudson interjected. "Hey, Rose, let me see if I have this straight. Yesterday afternoon, everything was fine with Audra. She had a new job that she seemed happy about. But she killed herself?"

"That's right," my grandmother said. "Makes you wonder if she was putting an act on for the lady at the shelter or if something changed after she dropped off the dogs."

"So how does Leif figure into all of this?" I asked.

Grandma sighed. "Your poor brother was the one to find Audra."

"Oh, no, that's awful," I said. "That couldn't have been easy."

"No, he's still shaken up. The lady from the animal shelter called Leif early this morning, asking if he could run by the farm and get the dogs' food. They're on a special diet and can't eat the regular kibble they have at the shelter."

Hudson furrowed his brow. "Why didn't Audra drop it off with the dogs?"

"Audra handed the shelter volunteer a couple of cans for the dogs' dinner. Then she said she'd bring in the rest of the food from the car, along with their squeaky toys and blankets. But when the volunteers went to get the dogs' breakfast, there wasn't any more canned food in the tote bag. That's when the lady at the shelter called Leif to ask if he could track down their food."

I bit back a smile. "So basically, Leif is an errand boy."

"Hopefully, he'll get back in the chief's good graces soon and get put back on regular police duty," my grandmother said.

"Don't hold your breath," I said, thinking about Chief Jeong's antagonism toward my brother. "What else did Leif say?"

"Well, first he called Sharon and asked her about the dog food. She gave him permission to go pick it up at the farm."

"Permission, huh?" I rolled my eyes. "Sounds like she thinks Leif is her errand boy, too."

Grandma made a tsk-tsk sound, before she filled us in on what Leif found when he went into Audra's cottage to look for the dog food. "When he walked in, he assumed it would be an empty house. But instead, he found the poor woman slumped over the kitchen table. Leif said she was cold to the touch. Apparently, she had been dead for hours."

"How did she kill herself?" Hudson asked. "Was it a gun?"

"No, they suspect it was an overdose. There was an empty bottle of prescription opiates next to her."

We were all silent for a while after that. What more was there to say? Two women were dead—one murdered, and one by their own hand. Eventually, my grandmother ended the call, saying she'd see us when we got back home. "I've got a pot roast in the slow cooker. I think your brother could use some comfort food for dinner, don't you? And I know Hudson likes it, too."

Hudson and I sat in the car, spending a good hour dissecting the shocking news that Audra had killed herself out of remorse for having taken Martha's life.

"I guess it was Scenario A2 after all," Hudson said as our conversation wound down. "Audra acted on her own. What's that they say about Occam's razor? The simplest explanation is usually the right one."

"This whole trip has been a colossal waste of time," I said. "And we hassled poor George for no reason."

"Hey, I was the good cop," Hudson teased. "I didn't hassle the guy."

I gave him a fond smile. "You really are a good guy, aren't you?"

Hudson squeezed my hand, and suggested we head back to Why. Maybe we should have spent a few more hours in Bismarck before heading back, so Hudson could see the capital city's attractions. But neither of us had the heart to sightsee. Solving the murder didn't bring us any joy or cause to celebrate. All it did was bring a sense of closure.

It was perfect timing, in a way. Tomorrow was the start of a new week. We could both go back to work with clear minds free of distraction, having put this investigation behind us.

That was the theory, anyway. For some reason, I

still had a feeling of unease. Something wasn't right. But what? I stared out the car window at the passing scenery and tried to figure it out. It wasn't until Hudson nudged me that I realized we had pulled up in front of my grandparents' house.

When I turned to look at him, Hudson gave me a gentle smile. "Guess this means we'll have more time to get ready for the book sale next weekend. You up for helping me this week?"

"Yep, I think we could both do with getting back to our boring normal."

Hudson's smile turned into a full-on grin. "You do realize that part of the book sale involves a naming contest for the town buffalo, don't you? I don't think you could get any further from boring and normal than that."

* * *

The heavenly smell of pot roast greeted us as we walked into my grandparents' house. "You're just in time," Grandma said as she scooped fluffy mashed potatoes into a serving bowl. "Grab yourself something to drink and sit down."

I handed Hudson a cola, and selected a can of ginger ale for myself. Grandpa and Leif were already seated at the kitchen table. Dr. McCoy was perched on the hutch, studiously ignoring the man who had run off to Bismarck and abandoned him.

"Hey, buddy," Hudson said to his cat. "Did you miss me?"

Dr. McCoy narrowed his eyes and let out a growl. A moment later, he hurled himself into Hudson's arms, purring madly.

"Guess everything is forgiven," I said, grabbing Hudson's can of pop from him, so that he could turn his full attention onto scratching the fluffy cat behind his ears. Chuckling, I turned to my grandparents. "How was kitty-sitting?"

"Your grandfather loved every minute of it," Grandma said. "The two of them like to play with twine. It was a match made in heaven."

"Maybe you should adopt a pet to keep you company when I move out," I suggested. Then I hastened to add, "Eventually." Could I really give up delicious meals like this pot roast? I glanced in Leif's direction. Of course, my younger brother turned up practically every other night for dinner. Maybe if I found a house close by, I could do the same thing.

"How about Martha's Pomeranians?" my brother asked, interrupting my thoughts. "They need a good home."

"Uff da," my grandmother said. "Dogs are too much work."

As she passed the platter of pot roast to my grandfather, he mumbled, "Maybe."

"Maybe what, Thor?" she asked him. "You can't seriously be suggesting we adopt those dogs."

Grandpa put some pot roast on his plate, tore a small piece off, and threw it on the floor. Dr. McCoy leaped out of Hudson's arms and rushed over to gobble up the morsel. Grandpa watched the cat for a few moments, before he turned his attention back to his own food.

"Those Pomeranians are on a special diet," Leif said. "You can't feed them scraps from the table."

"Okay," Grandpa said.

As my grandmother put her head in her hands, my brother and I smiled at each other.

"Who do you think is going to win this one?" Hudson asked us.

"Normally, I'd say Grandma," Leif said. "But Grandpa can be pretty stubborn when he has his heart set on something."

"Small, yippy dogs," I said. "Who would have thought that's what Grandpa would set his heart on?"

"The heart wants what the heart wants," Hudson said.

"Eat, now," Grandma ordered, obviously wanting to put an end to the dog discussion.

By mutual agreement, conversation over dinner steered away from pet adoption and Audra's death. Instead, we chatted about the Guinness Book of World Records (Grandpa still hadn't heard back), what the latest with Norma and Swede was (still a mystery, but Swede was seen at the florist buying red roses a couple of days ago), and the recent Major League

Baseball pitch clock changes (Grandpa was not a fan).

Once the plates were cleared and coffee with dessert were served, I asked Leif what was going to happen with the charges against Bobby Jorgenson.

"Should be dropped. I imagine they'll do the paperwork tomorrow morning," my brother said. "The suicide note made it clear that Audra killed Martha. Open and shut case."

"What exactly did the note say?" I asked.

"Here, I'll show you." Leif pulled out his phone and cautioned me. "Remember this is strictly off the record, okay?"

"Oh, so it wasn't an actual note," I said.

"What do you mean?" Hudson asked.

"This is a picture of Audra's laptop screen." I looked at Leif. "How did you get this? Wasn't her laptop password protected?"

"Nope," Leif said. "Kind of crazy in this day and age. When I jostled the table, her laptop came back on and the note was on the screen."

"I wonder why she didn't print it out," I mused.

Hudson shrugged. "We live in a digital age. It wouldn't surprise me if people left suicide notes in the form of reels on social media these days."

"Uff da," I said, subconsciously imitating my grandmother.

"What does the note say?" Hudson asked.

A chill went down my spine as I read Audra's last words out loud:

I can't forgive myself for ending Martha Lund's life. I wanted to ease her suffering, so I put arsenic in her sweetener. But now I recognize that I was wrong. I apologize to her family for what I've done.

"The poor woman," Hudson said. "To be at such a low point that she took her own life."

"But she didn't kill herself," I said slowly. "Audra was murdered."

The room fell silent for a few moments, Hudson asked, "Why do you think Audra was murdered?"

"For two reasons," I explained. "First, we know arsenic poisoning gave Martha some awful symptoms. If Audra was truly an 'angel of death,' she would have killed Martha in another way. Something painless and quick. She wouldn't have put Martha through a slow, agonizing death."

"Oh, that's a good point," Hudson said. "What's the other reason?"

"Because of her suicide note." I handed Leif's phone to him. "Take a look. It's pretty obvious she didn't write it."

"Geez, Thea. You're obsessed with murder." Leif snorted. "The note was on Audra's laptop. Of course she wrote it. Seriously, you need to get a life."

"I have a life," I snapped.

Leif rolled his eyes. "Sticking your nose in police business isn't a life."

"You're just jealous because the chief has you on dog poop detail and I'm the one who's *actually* investigating Martha's murder." I held up my index and middle fingers. "Oh, wait a minute. That's two murders."

"You need to work on your math skills. Audra killed herself." Leif waved his thumb in the air. "One murder, Thea. One."

"Um, actually, I think Thea is right," Hudson said quietly.

Leif snapped his head in the other man's direction. "What do you mean?"

Hudson handed Leif his phone back. "Look how Audra spelled 'recognize' and 'apologize' with a 'z.'"

Leif peered at the image of Audra's laptop, before he said, "Yeah, so?"

"Well, whoever wrote this note spelled those two words wrong," Hudson said.

Grandma motioned at Leif's phone. "Can I see that?"

While she was examining the photo, Leif turned back to Hudson. "Man, with all the books you read, I would have thought you'd know how to spell better," he said in a joking tone. "That's how 'recognize' and 'apologize' are spelled."

"That would be true if Audra wrote in American English," I pointed out. "But she's originally from Saint Marie in the Caribbean. It's a British Overseas Territory, so Audra would have used British English. They use an 's' instead of a 'z' as in R-E-C-O-G-N-I-S-E and A-P-O-L-O-G-I-S-E."

"But ... but ... she was living here," Leif spluttered. "She would have spelled those words the American way."

"She had only been living in the States for a couple of years," Hudson said. "Even if she used American spelling in work-related documents, she would naturally gravitate towards her native British spelling in personal matters."

"Like a suicide note. You can't get more personal than that," I said. "If you're about to end your life, you're going to fall back on the variety of English you've used since childhood."

"Good catch, Thea," my grandmother said to me.

"Now we just have to catch the real killer," I said.

"I suppose you know who it is," Leif said, his voice tight.

"Listen, you couldn't have known about the spelling," I said to my brother, empathizing with how he must be feeling. Having a sibling was a wonderful blessing most of the time. But when you feel one-upped by your brother or sister, it could sting. "I don't think you had ever spoken with Audra when she was alive, right?"

"No, I guess not," Leif admitted, his tone a little begrudging.

"You wouldn't have known about her background. Hudson and I happened to chat with her about it the day we were at Martha's checking on a book donation. She told us about growing up on Saint Marie and how they used British English. If it hadn't been for that conversation, I'm not sure we would have made the connection."

"Your sister isn't wrong," Grandma said to Leif. "Thea just happened to be in the right place at the right time."

"It seems like Thea is always in the right place at the right time," Leif admitted softly, his voice sounding like it did when we were little kids. As the younger sibling, my brother had struggled at times with the fact that I got to do things before him. Of course, on the flip side, I hated how he always seemed to get his way. Funny how childhood dynamics still reared their ugly head even in adulthood.

Hudson looked uncomfortable as the silence settled heavily in the air. Even my grandmother appeared at a loss as to how to lighten the mood.

Grandpa got up from the table and walked behind Leif's chair. Placing his hand on my brother's shoulder, he said simply, "Thea needs your help, son." He grabbed some scraps of twine that Dr. McCoy had been playing with and shuffled out to the barn.

"He's right," I said to Leif. "I do need your help. You're the only person who can help us figure out who the real murderer is."

Leif tilted his head. "How so?"

"I need you to set a trap," I said. "Tomorrow, you'll have to go to Swede's during the midday rush."

"So, you want me to eat lunch," Leif said slowly.

"How does a tuna fish sandwich solve a murder? Or should I have a grilled cheese instead?"

"Oh, it doesn't matter what you eat," I said. "The important thing is to pretend to be on the phone talking to a fellow police officer. You need to say something about how Audra left a handwritten note in one of the dresser drawers in her bedroom saying that she knew who really killed Martha."

"But she didn't leave a handwritten note," Leif pointed out.

"I know that, and you know that," I said. "But the killer doesn't."

Leif nodded. "Okay. What else does this imaginary note say?"

"In it, Audra says that she hid evidence in her house connecting the killer to Martha's murder," I explained. "You also need to say that the chief ordered a search of Audra's cottage to take place early the next morning. And make sure you speak loudly, that way everyone hears you."

"So, you're assuming the killer will be at Swede's at the exact same time Leif is there having a fake conversation on his phone?" Hudson asked.

"Well, that would be the ideal scenario. But even if they're not, you know how gossip spreads like wildfire in this town. The killer will hear about it in no time. They'll be desperate to find the evidence before the police do. When they turn up ..." I spread my hands out, indicating the obvious conclusion.

Leif frowned. "I'm not sure why you need my help. Why can't you be the one to start this rumor?"

"Because you're a police officer," I said. "The story will be a million times more believable if it comes from you."

"It all sounds great in theory, Thea." Leif leaned back in his chair, his hands behind his head. "But there's two problems with your plan."

"What's that?" I asked.

"The first is that it makes me look like I'm incompetent. What kind of police officer goes around talking about confidential information in public?" Before I could counter his argument, Leif shook his head. "Even if I was willing to look like a fool, the second problem is much bigger. My boss. If I go along with this and don't tell her, I'll lose my job."

"So, tell her," I said. "Tell her what we discovered about Audra's supposed suicide note. Once she realizes that Audra didn't kill herself and the real murderer is still out there, she'll get on board with our plan."

Leif chuckled. "Sure, that'll work. Chief Jeong will love to hear about one of the Olson women meddling in things. Besides, Audra's death hasn't even been officially ruled a suicide. The chief is all about following procedure. And this is *not* by the book."

"I don't need any credit," I said. "Tell the chief that you figured out the spelling discrepancy. Maybe she'll take you more seriously then."

"I'm not going to do that," Leif said. "You figured it out, fair and square."

"Credit or no credit, you better go call the chief and tell her what's going on." Grandma pursed her lips. "As much as I hate to say it, the ball's in her court. She'll need to figure out what to do next."

"Okay, wish me luck." Leif got to his feet and grabbed his phone off the table. "Wait a minute. Before I call her, who *murdered* Martha and Audra? You never said."

"That's because I don't know," I said simply.

"Darn it." Hudson ran his fingers through his hair. "I was hoping you'd cracked the case."

I gave him a wry smile. "Well, the good news is I think we have it narrowed down to three people—Ray, Sharon, and Cassidy. According to Bobby, two people came to Martha's the afternoon she died. One of them was Ray, but we don't know who the other person was. I think it was Sharon or Cassidy. Of course, that is assuming George's story checks out."

"What's George's story?" Leif asked.

"George said that the security footage at his shop will show he was at work Monday afternoon," I said. "That means he wasn't the person Bobby saw. Also, he was at the bank in Williston on Tuesday when I overheard Cassidy talking to a guy about stealing books from Martha."

Leif sat back at the table, his phone call to the chief forgotten. "If Cassidy wasn't talking to George, who was she talking to?"

"Ray," I said. "George and Ray are both originally from the south and have similar accents."

Hudson held up his hand. "They probably sound similar to you, but someone from the south might have been able to distinguish them. George is from the Carolinas and Ray is from Texas, right?"

"Sure, that's a fair point, but you have to remember, I was fixated on the fact that the person Cassidy was talking with was a book collector. Naturally, that made me think of George. But Ray would have been interested in books as well, provided they were a specific type of book."

"Ah, books about gardening," Hudson said.

I nodded. "That's right. Cassidy was there when we were going through Martha's books at the library. Those green leather-bound ones were about gardening. She knew they were valuable, so she stole them to give to Ray."

Leif leaned forward. "So, you think Ray and Cassidy were working together?"

"Cassidy was a cleaner at Martha's house," I said. "Ray was desperate to get his hands on Martha's prize seeds. He might have had a little arrangement with Cassidy. If she could find the seeds for him, he'd pay her. The gardening books were just icing on the top."

I paused for a moment when Dr. McCoy jumped on the table and knocked over my cup. While I cleaned up the mess, my grandmother got another pot of

French roast brewing. Once the cat was situated in Hudson's lap and we all had a fresh cup of coffee in hand, I explained how there were a couple of scenarios to consider. "Ray and Cassidy's little arrangement was either just about stealing stuff or it was more nefarious ... and Ray had Cassidy put arsenic in Martha's sweetener."

"You do love your little scenarios," Hudson joked.

"Scenarios are fun," I admitted. "It's part of puzzling out the mystery."

"Why would Ray have gone to Martha's the day she died?" Leif asked. "He knew he wasn't welcome there."

"Martha had fired Cassidy," I said. "So, she didn't have access anymore to look for the seeds. He was getting desperate about this year's county fair, so maybe he decided to take a more direct approach. Perhaps he was going to try to intimidate Martha and force her into giving them to him. But he lucked out. When he went into the kitchen, Martha was dead, and her secret recipe box was sitting on the table with the packet of seeds in it. He grabbed them and took off."

"The big question is, did he also take the container with the poisoned sweetener to cover his tracks," Hudson said.

I took a sip of my coffee before I said, "You know, in a way, I feel sorry for the killer. If Bobby hadn't found that old rat poison bottle in the shed and brought it into Martha's kitchen, I'm not sure anyone would have suspected she had been poisoned with arsenic."

"What do you mean?" Grandma asked.

"Think about it," I said. "An old woman known to be suffering from a terminal disease was found dead. Would the police have tested the contents of Martha's coffee if they hadn't seen the rat poison bottle on the counter? Would the medical examiner have run tests to determine levels of arsenic? Maybe not. They might have just attributed the cause of death to a massive heart attack and left it at that."

"It probably didn't help either that a lot of law enforcement officers were on the scene that day," Leif said. "If there hadn't been so many of us milling around the kitchen, the rat poison bottle might have gone unnoticed."

"Why were there so many of you guys there, anyway?" Hudson asked.

"Turf war," Leif said cynically. "When one of the richest people in the state dies, both the local police and the sheriff's office want to make their presence known, even if they think they died of natural causes. And the more officers you have, the more important your agency must be."

My grandmother cleared her throat and added, "So, we've talked about Ray and Cassidy. What about Sharon?"

"Sharon has always been the most obvious suspect," I said. "She had access to her aunt's house and could have easily added the arsenic to the sweetener. Assuming Sharon is the other person Bobby saw at Martha's that day, my money's on her."

"You said Bobby should be released from jail tomorrow, right?" my grandmother asked Leif.

"I'd be surprised if he wasn't," Leif said. "I can find out for sure and let you know."

Grandma nodded. "Good, because I'm planning on picking up the poor boy and finding out exactly who he saw. Then we can narrow down the suspect list and put Thea's plan into action."

Leif waved his phone in the air. "I still need to call Chief Jeong."

"Go on," Grandma said to him. "We'll have some ice cream when you're done."

"I have a feeling I might need more than ice cream after this call." Leif frowned. "Got any whiskey?"

"Don't be silly. You're going to need a clear head to put this trap in place." Grandma smiled at him. "But I'll be sure to put an extra scoop in your bowl."

CHAPTER 15
DON'T FORGET THE COOKIES

The next morning, while I stayed back at the house working, my grandmother went and picked up Bobby Jorgenson from the county jail. I was in the middle of a video call when Grandma sent a group text with the information we had all been waiting for—Sharon had been the other person Bobby had seen at Martha's that day, not Cassidy.

I have to confess to not being as focused on my business call as I should have been. Instead, I was glued to my phone as the texts flew back and forth between Grandma, Leif, Hudson, and me.

After a disastrous call with Chief Jeong the previous night, Leif was out of the picture. The chief had scoffed at the idea that Audra hadn't written the suicide note. She had been adamant that Leif needed to focus on his K-9 duties and stop poking around in things that weren't his business. In her mind, Martha's murder was solved. Audra had done it, plain and simple. She also had a few choice words to say about the Olson women, which Leif wisely paraphrased when he relayed the conversation to us.

Setting the trap for Martha's true killer was now down to Hudson and me. It was actually going to work out better this way. Instead of having Leif do a scattergun approach to spreading the rumor around town that the police were planning to search Audra's cottage, Hudson and I were going to be more targeted. We agreed that I would go to the Beauty Bucket this afternoon while Sharon was working and casually mentioning Audra's handwritten note claiming to have hidden evidence pointing at the real murderer. Ray would be at the library for a Gardening Club sub-committee meeting in the morning, so Hudson was in charge of making sure he caught wind of our little fictitious story about Audra.

Once our plans were settled, I got back to work for a few hours. After wrangling with some spreadsheets, setting up a client survey, and writing up a coaching feedback report, I headed into town.

When I walked into the Beauty Bucket, Artifice practically pounced on me.

"Perfect timing, hon. I just had a cancellation so I can squeeze you in." She steered me toward a chair talking a mile a minute about the latest trends in eyebrow artistry. "Once we get these roots of yours touched up, I'll tackle your brows. You're not scared of razors, are you?"

Like the last time I had been in the salon, the place was deserted. Artifice's hard-sell approach was probably scaring away potential customers. "Actually, I was hoping Sharon was in," I said. "I never did get that hair appointment with her rescheduled. Maybe she's got some time now?"

Artifice stared at me for a few moments as she chomped on her gum, and then yelled out, "Sharon, got a customer for you."

Sharon popped her head out of the back room, a bright smile plastered across her face. "Be there in a sec." Once she realized I was the customer in question, the expression on her face hardened. "Oh, it's you."

I gave her a cheery wave. "I was hoping you could squeeze me in for a trim."

Either professionalism or the desperate need for a paying customer got the better of her. She gave me a pleasant look and pointed to her station. "Of course, Thea. Anything for you."

After agreeing that a half an inch off should do, Sharon shampooed my hair. Next she assessed my ends, got out her scissors, and silently set to work. I tried to engage her in conversation, but she only gave me one or two-word answers. Thankfully, Artifice gave me the opening I needed.

"Any word on when the memorial service for your aunt is going to take place?" she asked Sharon. "Oh, and is your brother in town yet?"

"Yes, he got in yesterday." Sharon let out a deep sigh. "He's still the same jerk he always was. I keep telling myself that I only have to put up with him for a few days and then I don't ever need to see him again."

Artifice settled into the chair next to Sharon's station. "Why? What did he do?"

"We went to the lawyer's this morning and the first thing Robert did was hit on the receptionist. The girl is like thirty years younger than him, and she was wearing a wedding ring. But did that stop him? No. Of course not. He's a pig, like all men."

"What did the receptionist do?" Artifice asked.

"She humored him. But I could tell it was only because she was at work. If Robert had hit on her at a bar, I'm sure she would have had something else to say." I jerked my head away as Sharon waved around her scissors for emphasis. "And get this. When the receptionist went to tell the lawyer that we were there, Robert reached into her handbag and pulled out her wallet."

Artifice gasped. "He was going to steal her wallet?"

"Yep, like I told you, same old Robert. I told him I'd scream bloody murder if he didn't put it back." Sharon started trimming my hair again for a few moments. After making sure the ends were even, she turned back to Artifice. "Do you know what the worst part is? My aunt split her estate between the two of us. After everything he did, she left him half of everything she owned."

"Wow, she must have had a change of heart," Artifice said.

"She had told me that's what she was planning to do. We fought about it a lot. She kept trash talking my brother, so I thought I had talked some sense into her." Sharon set the scissors down on the vanity and ran her fingers through my hair. "But if you're dying of cancer, I guess that changes things."

"I can see your aunt not wanting to go to her grave with regrets," Artifice said gently.

Sharon gave a mirthless laugh as she reached for the blow dryer. "Honestly, until we went to the lawyer, I wasn't sure who she had left her estate to. I wouldn't have been surprised if she gave all her money away to the high school marching band. My aunt did like to keep people on their toes with her little mind games."

Worried that the conversation would end once Sharon started drying my hair, I piped up. "I guess it must be a shock finding out that Audra didn't kill your aunt."

Sharon locked eyes with me in the mirror. "What are you talking about? Audra left a suicide note."

"But I heard that's not the only note she left. Promise you'll keep this between you and me?" After both women nodded, I said dramatically, "The police found another note in Audra's dresser drawer. In it, she said that she had evidence pointing to the real killer hidden somewhere in the cottage."

"No way," Artifice said, snapping her gum. "This is like one of those mystery shows I watch. There's all these twists and turns and you never know—"

Sharon cut her off, saying, "I don't believe it. In fact, if you don't mind, I'd rather not hear any more about my aunt's death. It's hard enough having to deal with my brother and finalizing the funeral arrangements."

"Sorry. There's a rumor that the police are going to do a search of the cottage early tomorrow morning to find the evidence," I said quickly. "Aren't you curious about what they'll find?"

"You don't really want a blow dry, do you? I think your hair will look better if you let it dry naturally." Sharon turned to Artifice. "Mind ringing Thea up? I need to take care of something in the back."

"Sure, no problem, hon," Artifice said to Sharon. After taking my smock off, and shaking it out, Artifice told me she'd meet me at the register. As I grabbed my things, I heard Artifice thank someone for bringing over coffee. "You're an angel. I could really use a caffeine boost."

I looked up and saw George balancing a cup carrier in one hand and a bag of pastries in the other. He gave me a curt nod and turned back to Artifice. "I've got your usuals. Skinny raspberry latte for you and a cappuccino for Sharon. I threw in a couple of blondies since it's Sharon's first day back at work."

George's face flushed as Artifice kissed him on the cheek, and I wondered if it might be the start of one of those 'opposites attract' love stories. I waited until George had gone before approaching the front desk. After the disastrous scene at his cousin's bookstore in Bismarck, I think it was going to be a long time before our relationship returned to a usual easygoing friendship.

But that was something to worry about later. It was time to head to Audra's cottage and wait for the killer to turn up. The question was—would it be Sharon or Ray?

* * *

"How long do you think we're going to have to wait?" Hudson asked me later that night.

Based on the assumption that the killer wouldn't show up until after dark, we had been hiding in the greenhouse next to Audra's cottage since five o'clock. The vantage point gave us a clear line of sight to the driveway and front door, as well as providing a much welcome shelter from the bracing winds of a nearing storm.

There had been a debate as to whether it would be better to hide in the cottage, but in the end, we both agreed that it was too risky to confront the killer.

Instead, we planned to take photographs of whoever entered the cottage, and then call the police to report a break-in. Hopefully, the police would catch them in the act of tearing the place apart, and Chief Jeong would be forced to admit that the case should be reopened.

However, there was a serious flaw in our plan. If Sharon turned out to be the killer, she could easily argue her aunt's property belonged to her, she had every right to be there, and that she was merely taking inventory of what was in the cottage. That's why I was secretly hoping Ray turned out to be the murderer. It would make life so much simpler.

Hudson nudged me. "What time is it?"

I glanced at my phone. "Eight. Pass me the chips, will you?"

Hudson reached into the cooler my grandmother had packed us. "You're going to need snacks if you're on a stakeout all night," she had said as she tucked ham and Swiss sandwiches and potato chips into the cooler before we left. "It's important to keep your strength up."

"I'm more worried about not having any place to pee than I am about starving to death," I had told her. "Guys have it so much easier in that department."

"Hmm ... good point," she had said. "Maybe I should put only one can of ginger ale in here for you."

"Someone's coming," Hudson whispered, jolting me back to our current situation—crouched on the compacted dirt floor of Martha's greenhouse desperately needing to pee as a killer slowly pulled their car into a parking spot in front of Audra's house.

"Hurry up, take pictures," I said in hushed tones.

Hudson crawled forward on his belly, snapping pictures through the glass door. The camera and telephoto lens Hudson had checked out from the library was supposed to be able to capture images in low light from a distance, even without a flash.

I snaked behind Hudson, pressing my body against a stack of large terracotta pots. Adrenaline coursed through my body, causing me to shake. Worried I was going to knock the pots down, I inched closer to Hudson, relaxing slightly as I felt the warmth of his body next to mine.

"Wait a minute," I said sharply as a man got out of the car. "That's not the killer. It's Leif."

I got to my feet and rushed out of the greenhouse. Grabbing my brother's arm, I yanked him toward me. "What the heck are you doing here?"

"Do you really think I'd let my sister put herself in danger by lying in wait for a murderer?" Leif said.

"Hudson is with me," I retorted.

"Let me rephrase that." As Leif placed his hands on his hips, I noted that he wasn't dressed in his uniform and the vehicle he had pulled up in was his old Honda Civic, not a squad car. "Do you think I would let my sister and her unarmed companion put themselves in danger waiting for a killer to show up?"

I took a deep breath, letting it out slowly. "As much as I appreciate what you're trying to do, I don't want you to jeopardize your job. Leave this to us."

Leif shook his head. "Yeah, no. Not gonna happen. Besides, Grandma forgot to pack oatmeal raisin cookies in the cooler. She'd kill me if I didn't bring them to you."

As my brother thrust the bag of cookies in my hand, Hudson suggested Leif hide his car. "We parked mine behind the barn, so we don't spook our mystery guest off."

"Makes sense," Leif said. "I'll be back in a jiff."

While we waited in the greenhouse for Leif to return, I handed Hudson one of the cookies. "These are good," he said between bites. "Chewy and crunchy at the same time. How does your grandmother do that?"

"I'm not sure. Maybe I'll ask her to teach me how to make them." I set the bag of cookies on top of the cooler and peered out the door. "That idiot, he's driving back up here. What part of 'go hide your car behind the barn' didn't he understand?"

I marched back outside, tapping my foot on the gravel as I waited for Leif to park his Civic again. But as the car door opened, I realized this wasn't my brother's vehicle. When I saw who the driver was, I gasped. "Damian, what are you doing here?"

George's cousin got out of the car and drew himself up to his full imposing height. As he took a step toward me, he said, "I could ask you the same thing."

"I'm, um ..." my voice trailed off as Damian pulled a knife out of his jacket and brandished it at me.

"Let me guess, you were waiting for me to show," Damian said. "I told George this was a set-up, but he insisted you were too stupid for that. Guess he was wrong, wasn't he?"

"Run, Thea!" Hudson yelled. I whipped around and saw him standing in the doorway of the greenhouse, holding a piece of metal pipe in his hands. His eyes locked with mine as he urged me again to run. But my feet wouldn't move. Fear froze me in place despite the danger I knew was looming behind me.

"I should have known you'd bring your librarian boyfriend with you," Damian sneered as he wrapped one of his arms around my waist and dragged me back toward him. I struggled to get away, but stilled when I felt the tip of the knife blade against my throat. "Drop the pipe, buddy, or else your girlfriend is going to start bleeding."

Hudson gulped, clearly reluctant to let go of the only weapon he had. "I'm sorry," he whispered to me as the pipe clattered to the ground.

Damian relaxed his grip around my waist slightly, but he still held the knife close to my throat. If I was going to die, I at least wanted to know why.

"Cassidy was telling the truth, wasn't she?" I asked with more confidence than I felt. "Sharon was the mastermind behind everything. She paid George to kill her aunt, and you were part of it. And that's why you're here. After I told Sharon about Audra leaving evidence behind in the cottage, she sent you to find it before the police did."

"Sharon? A mastermind? Oh, please. The woman is a hairdresser." Damian gave a brittle laugh. "She didn't have anything to do with this. I'm the one who came up with the plan. I told George that if we got rid of Martha, we could get our hands on her book collection for a song. Sharon is too stupid to know its true value. We'd come in, offer to take them off her hands. It'd be one less thing for her to deal with. Then we'd resell them and make a fortune."

I looked over at Hudson, standing helplessly as Damian told us how George had put the arsenic in Martha's sweetener before he gave it to her. "All we had to do was wait until she died. She was old and frail. We didn't expect it to take very long, and it didn't."

"All that experience as an international aid worker came in handy, didn't it?" I asked. "You had seen how arsenic poisoning worked firsthand."

I shuddered as Damian leaned down, his hot breath in my ear as he whispered, "I'm going to have to come up with another way to kill you and your boyfriend. Arsenic takes too much time. And I can't use pills again, not like I did with Audra."

"So, you killed Audra," I said flatly. "You made her overdose on those opiates."

"Yeah, it wasn't my first choice," Damian said. "But she didn't have a gun. If she did, I would have made it look like she shot herself."

"Where did you get the pills?" I asked, stalling for time. "Were they Audra's?"

"No, they belonged to me. It's a little sideline of mine with a doctor I know. He writes fake prescriptions. I get folks to fill them. Then, um, how do I put this ... basically, I redistribute the pills to other people." Damian chuckled as though he was proud of himself.

"Basically, you're running a pill mill."

The bitterness in my voice was a mistake. "When I'm done with you, you're going to wish I forced you to swallow a bunch of pills like I did with Audra," Damian said. "You only have yourself to blame for her death, you know. If you hadn't stuck your big fat nose in our business, asking all those questions in Bismarck, I wouldn't have had to do it. But with the police breathing down our neck, I needed someone to take the blame for Martha's death. A stranger in a small town? The perfect fall guy. Or gal, should I say?"

"Two people are dead because of your greed," I said, spitting out each word like a bitter pill. "This was all because of money."

"Don't act so high and mighty, sweetheart." Damian abruptly lowered the knife. With his arm still grasping my waist, he pushed me forward toward Hudson. "Tell your boyfriend to pop the trunk of my car and get inside."

Instead of relaying Damian's command, I said, "No way. If you're going to kill us, do it here."

Hudson's eyes grew wide, but I saw them flicker slightly to the side. I was hoping that I understood what he was trying to convey. I needed to get away from Damian. A pile of pavers sat in front of me, probably something Bobby had been moving as part of his work in Martha's garden. If I could somehow maneuver our way over there ... but how?

Luckily, I didn't need to figure it out. Damian nudged me in that direction in order for him to confront Hudson. I managed to make it look like I slipped. As I started to fall, Damian yanked me back up. In the process, we tripped over the pavers and tumbled to the ground.

"Thea, run!" a man's voice called. Only this time, it wasn't Hudson. Leif was standing behind me, aiming his gun directly at Damian. I didn't need to be told twice, quickly darting away into Hudson's arms.

As sirens blared in the distance, I had a feeling I was about to have another encounter with Chief Jeong. Only this time, I think even she'd have to admit that our meddling had paid off.

CHAPTER 16
AND THE BUFFALO'S NAME IS . . .

The following weekend, the book sale at the library was in full swing. After Damian and George's arrests for the murders of Martha Lund and Audra Bordey, people were eager for an excuse to congregate and gossip about what had happened in Why. The fact that the weather was sunny and warm meant that we were able to hold the event outdoors. The tables of books lining the sidewalk in front of the library, the vendor booths and food trucks in the parking lot, and the high school show choir performing on a stage on the lawn lent a festive atmosphere.

On Saturday, a record number of books were sold, raising significantly more money than in any previous year the event had been held. By the time Sunday afternoon rolled around, the stock of books left for people to buy was fairly limited. But a big crowd was still in attendance, no doubt due to the fact that the town buffalo's name was about to be revealed.

As Hudson tallied up the final results from the naming contest, I hung out with my grandmother and Leif at one of the picnic tables.

"How's it going with the chief?" I asked my brother. "Any signs of a thawing in relations?"

"I think it's going to be a while." Leif sighed. "She still has me on K-9 duty."

"Uff da," Grandma said. "If it hadn't been for you, Damian would have killed Thea and Hudson, and then he and George would have escaped town. Is that really what Chief Jeong wanted? For two murderers to go free?"

Leif shook his head. "No, of course not. She admitted that she was wrong about Audra's suicide note. But that doesn't mean she's not upset about the 'Olson women and the librarian' meddling in police business."

"The Olson women and the librarian." I chuckled. "That sounds like a bad sitcom."

Grandma grinned. "We prefer to be called the Three Investigators."

"I wish this was a sitcom," Leif said to me. "Instead, my life at the police station is more like some sort of melodrama these days."

"I'm sorry, dear." Grandma squeezed Leif's hand. "I realize that we put you in a difficult position."

"Grandma's right," I said to my brother. "Our meddling might have helped solve the case, but it wasn't fair to you."

"Things will get better. I promise you that," Grandma said as she gave Leif's hand one final squeeze. "They always do."

"I hope you're right." Leif took a sip of his cola. "I don't think they're going to get better for Cassidy and Ray anytime soon, though."

"Why? What have you heard—" I started to ask, but I stopped myself. "Sorry, you shouldn't tell us confidential information."

Leif waved a hand in the air. "Nah, it's not confidential anymore. I actually heard Norma and Swede talking about it."

"You did? When was this?" I asked.

"Earlier this morning," my brother said. "I went into Swede's to get some coffee and—"

My grandmother leaned forward, her eyes wide with curiosity. "Norma is back working at the diner?"

Leif took another sip of his drink before saying, "Uh-huh."

"You sound like Grandpa with that one-word answer," I said. "Dish the dirt already. Are Norma and Swede a couple? How did they act with each other?"

"I thought you wanted to hear about Cassidy and Ray," Leif said. "Not discuss Norma and Swede's love life."

"Personally, I'd like to hear about both," Grandma

admitted, a sly smile on her face. "Start with Cassidy and Ray, then we'll move on to the romance side of things."

I wrinkled my nose. "It's kind of weird thinking about Norma and Swede in that way."

My grandmother shushed me, before she turned back to Leif. "Go on."

"Okay. Well, as you know, the police hauled Cassidy and Ray in for questioning. Cassidy kept spinning story after story, each one more elaborate than the last."

"Like she did when she claimed to have overheard George talking to his cousin about Sharon hiring him to kill her aunt." I tapped my lips with my fingers. "Do you think there was any basis to that story? Had she actually overheard George and Damian talking about murdering Martha and then embellished it to implicate Sharon?"

"That's exactly what happened," Leif said. "They finally got that out of her after her lawyer told her things would go better if she stopped with the lies and started telling the truth."

"So, what was the truth?" my grandmother asked.

Leif pointed at me. "Just like Thea suspected. Ray was paying Cassidy to look for the prize seeds at Martha's when she was a cleaner there. Stealing the gardening books and giving them to Ray was opportunistic."

"What's going to happen to her?" I asked.

He shrugged. "Don't know. She's been in trouble with the law before, so that won't help. But they might take into account the fact that she was just trying get money to help her uncle out."

"What about Ray?" my grandmother asked.

"Ah, that's where things get interesting. Not only was he the mastermind of the so-called 'green thumb' racket, but he also took the container of arsenic-laden sweetener from Martha's kitchen."

I furrowed my brow. "Ray? Why? He wasn't involved in poisoning Martha."

"No, he wasn't," my brother agreed. "As we know, when he went to Martha's that day and found her dead in the kitchen, he stole the packets of seeds that were in a recipe box on the table. He saw the enameled candy container with a flower pattern on it and quickly grabbed it, hoping Martha had stashed some other seed packets in there."

"You're kidding," I said. "I bet he was disappointed when he discovered what was really inside."

"Yes, and thankfully, he didn't try the sweetener. He drinks his coffee black." Leif slurped down the rest of his cola before he told us that he had run into Bobby Jorgenson at Swede's too.

My grandmother tilted her head to one side. "How's the poor boy doing?"

"He seemed okay," Leif said. "He just got a new job at the roller-skating rink."

I burst out laughing. "Really? Doing what?"

"Teaching a skating class." Leif held up his hands. "Apparently, Bobby is a really good skater. I guess you never know about people."

Thinking about how mild-mannered bookstore owner George had turned out to be a murderer, I nodded. "I guess you don't."

"Let's get back to Swede and Norma," my grandmother said after a beat.

Leif grinned. "Okay, here's what I know. It's not much really. Norma is back waitressing like she never left, and Swede is still flipping burgers and barking orders. But when Norma went into the kitchen to grab something, I saw Swede pat her on the behind. Then she swatted him on his behind and the two of them started giggling."

We spent a few more minutes dissecting Norma and Swede's burgeoning relationship, when I said, "What's Grandpa doing with Martha's dogs?" I pointed at a bench near the entrance to the library. My grandfather was sitting in the middle with a Pomeranian nestled on either side of him. As I watched him open a piece of mail, I said to my grandmother, "Don't tell me he adopted them?"

"Yes, it's true." My grandmother sighed. "We're now the proud owners of those little cutie-pies. What can I say? It makes Thor happy."

Grandpa tucked the letter he had been reading into the front pocket of his overalls and helped the dogs get off the bench to the ground. He looked around.

When he spotted us, he gave a wave before the three of them shuffled over to where we were sitting.

I nudged my grandmother. "Wow, I'd say they make him really happy. Grandpa has a huge grin on his face."

"You're right," my grandmother said. "How odd."

The dogs strained at their leashes as they neared, eager to greet us. While I cuddled with one of the dogs, and Leif played tug of war with the other, Grandpa handed Grandma the letter.

She gasped after she read it. "Oh, Thor, this is wonderful news."

"What is it?" Leif asked.

"The Guinness Book of World Records is coming to Why to see your grandfather's giant ball of twine," she said. "They're going to measure it and decide if it's the world record holder."

"Oh, my gosh," I whispered to Leif. "They're hugging. In public."

Leif smiled at me. "Uh, I think Grandpa just gave Grandma a peck on the cheek."

I grinned back at him. "First Norma and Swede getting together, and now PDA from our grandparents ... love really is in the air."

* * *

As I was walking over to the food trucks to get a lemonade, a man's voice crackled over the loudspeakers. "Can I have everyone's attention, please? Please make your way over to the stage. We'll be announcing the official name of Why's resident buffalo in ten minutes."

I stifled a laugh when I realized who the speaker was—Doc had dressed up as Paul Bunyan, complete with a black cap on his head, a red and black plaid shirt, blue pants, red socks, and black boots. Considering the real Paul Bunyan was reputed to be over eighteen feet tall, having the nearly seven foot tall former basketball player dress up as the famous lumberjack was an inspired choice.

Fortunately, the line was short at the Citrus Shack truck. I grabbed my drink and rushed over to join my family near the stage. As we were waiting, my brother and I taunted each other about what name was going to be the winner.

"Twinkie," Leif said.

"A buffalo named after a snack cake. Never," I said. "It's going to be Bufford."

A woman behind us said, "I hope Babe wins."

Leif turned around. "After the pig?"

"No," she replied, pointing at the stage. "Babe as in Paul Bunyan's companion, Babe the Blue Ox."

"Well, that would be better than Twinkie." I elbowed my brother. "Anything would be better than Twinkie."

Our grandmother shushed us. "I want to hear what Paul ... I mean, Doc has to say."

"If I could ask our library director to join me on stage with the official results," Doc said.

Hudson walked up on stage carrying a sealed envelope. But before he handed it to Doc, he whispered something in the other man's ear. Doc nodded, and turned back to the audience.

"Before we reveal the buffalo's name, there's someone who would like to say a few words." Doc motioned to someone. "Come on up, dear."

"Is that Sharon?" I asked Leif.

"Looks like it," he said.

As the petite woman briskly walked across the stage, I noticed her previously brown hair was now strawberry blonde. She grabbed the microphone from Doc, and then pivoted to face the audience. "Thank you ..." she said, her voice uncertain. Her smile faltered for a moment before she seemed to regain her confidence. "Thank you for letting me speak to everyone this afternoon. The death of my beloved aunt and the break-up of my, um, marriage, has caused me to reevaluate things. It's also given me an opportunity to reconnect with my brother. We've had some good conversations, and some difficult ones."

Sharon paused and looked down at the stage. After a moment, she cleared her throat and continued. "My brother and I don't agree on everything, that's for sure. But one thing we do agree on is wanting to do more for the community. As a result, we've decided to donate my aunt's book collection to Why's library."

As everyone applauded, I wondered how much Sharon had really changed. Sure, she had a new hair color, and her generosity was unquestioned, but was the hard, calculating woman I had known still there deep inside? Was this all a ploy? Then I shook my head, reminding myself that we all have the capacity for personal growth. Grace waits in broken places for us all.

* * *

A few hours later, I was helping Hudson clean up from the book sale. Almost everyone else had gone, and just a few books were left to box up and bring inside the library. When I picked up a tattered book that had fallen on the ground, I started chuckling.

"What's so funny?" Hudson asked.

"It's a mystery about a robbery at a roller derby." I showed Hudson the cover of the book. "It reminded me of Bobby Jorgenson's new job. I heard he's going to be teaching a skating class."

"Good for him," Hudson said. "Oh, that reminds me. You promised that you'd go to the roller-skating rink with me. Are you free on Friday night?"

"Sure," I said brightly.

"We could go to dinner afterward," Hudson suggested.

"Are you asking me out on, um ... Is this a, um, a ..." I looked down at the ground as my voice trailed off.

"A date? Yes, it is." Hudson put his fingers underneath my chin, lifting it up so that he could look at me. He gave me a shy smile, before saying quickly, "Unless you don't want it to be. Did I misread things? Are we just friends?"

I took a deep breath and let it out slowly. "I'd like to be more than friends. But are you sure you're ready to start dating?"

"I'm ready to start dating you." Hudson took my hands in his and caressed them gently. "We just need to take it slow, okay?"

We stood there for a few moments in that weirdly awkward place in time and space where you wonder if he's going to kiss you or if you should kiss him. But before I could find out which one of us was going to be the brave one, I caught sight of a mass of shaggy brown fur out of the corner of my eye. Clearly, the town buffalo didn't care if he was interrupting a romantic interlude.

Letting go of Hudson's hands; I turned toward the buffalo. "What are you holding in your mouth, Bufford?"

"You just love saying his new name." Hudson chuckled. "You practically screamed when I announced that your choice was the winner of the contest."

"What can I say? It's a good name and it suits him." I pointed at Bufford. "You realize he's got a book in his mouth. He's getting drool all over it."

Hudson took a step forward, and grinned. "It's a Three Investigators book. Go figure."

"Gosh, I hope he's not trying to tell us something. I could use a break before our next case."

"Same," Hudson agreed as he tried to grab the book from Bufford. I think the buffalo thought it was some sort of game, like how dogs play with their favorite toys. He snorted, pawed at the ground with his hoof, and tore off across the parking lot. He kept looking back over his shoulder, taunting Hudson as he chased after him.

"Bufford," I said, laughing to myself as I watched the comical scene. "That does have a nice ring. So much better than Twinkie."

"Hey, don't get too cocky, lady," I heard Edgar call out from behind me. When I turned around, I saw him perched on the sill of an open window. "You're not going to win every contest."

"Just as long as I win the important ones," I said with a grin.

Edgar rolled one of his eyes, while keeping the other one firmly fixed on me. "You know I have a bone to pick with you, lady."

I arched an eyebrow. "What's that?"

"You bailed on our book club," he huffed.

"I was kind of busy with the investigation." I bit back a smile. How many people could say they had been chastened by a reptile for not showing up to a book club meeting?

"You mean floundering with the investigation." Edgar glared at me. "Listen, lady, if you had showed up for our discussion of *Strong Poison*, I could have given you some pointers about the investigation. I'm your guide, after all, remember?"

I thought about this for a minute, and held up my hands in submission. "You're right. But you have to understand, this whole 'guide' thing is new to me. Not to mention, this 'investigating murders' thing."

Wanting to change the subject, I motioned to where the chameleon was sitting. "I thought you couldn't go out of the building."

"I'm not outside, dummy." Edgar tapped the windowsill with one of his claws. "This is part of the library. I like to enjoy the sunshine when I can, like everyone else. And this is the only way I can do it."

I almost felt sorry for the reptile, confined to the building because of the weird workings of whatever magic governed his role as my so-called guide. When I said as much, he scoffed, "Trust me lady, unless you're going to take me back to New York City, I don't have any desire to leave this library. Although ..."

"Although what?" I asked.

Edgar flicked his tongue out, trying to catch a fly. When he missed, he turned back to me. "We might have to figure out a way for you to transport me to your grandfather's barn. Not quite yet, but soon."

"What are you talking about?" I asked. Of course, the only response I got was the familiar whooshing noise and flashing light of Edgar disappearing.

THE CARD CATALOG

One of the things I love about writing a library themed cozy mystery series is sharing my love of all things bookish. Think of this as your personal "card catalog" of the books mentioned in **Poisoned by the Book**.

As you can imagine, not only do I write mysteries, I love to read them as well. Classic mysteries, such as **The Hound of the Baskervilles** by Arthur Conan Doyle, will always hold a special place in my heart. Arthur Conan Doyle's Sherlock Holmes books were some of the first "grown-up" mysteries that I read. I really enjoy revisiting them periodically over the years.

Strong Poison by Dorothy L. Sayers is another classic mystery I've read multiple times. The banter between the detective duo of Lord Peter Wimsey and Harriet Vane as they solve mysteries is so much fun, and watching their relationship develop over the course of the series is an added bonus.

Of course, you can't talk about classic mysteries and not mention Agatha Christie. If you enjoy collections of short stories, **The Thirteen Problems** featuring Miss Marple is one you'll want to check out.

In addition to classic mysteries, I've included a couple of other classics in this card catalog: a dystopian novel and a play. **Brave New World** by Aldous Huxley was published in 1932 and describes a futuristic World

State whose citizens are carefully controlled and psychologically manipulated. The title of Huxley's novel comes from a speech by Miranda in Shakespeare's *The Tempest*.

Huxley isn't the only person who has drawn on Shakespeare to title their works. Gabrielle Zevin references Macbeth's soliloquy about his empty life in the title of her book, *Tomorrow, and Tomorrow, and Tomorrow*. Did you ever pick up a book at the library because of all the hype around it but didn't expect to really like it? That's what I did with *Tomorrow, and Tomorrow, and Tomorrow*. Turns out not only did I like it, I loved it! That's what's great about libraries— you can try out books for free that end up surprising you.

If you're looking for a light-hearted read that will have you laughing out loud, check out J. Maarten Troost's memoir, *The Sex Lives of Cannibals Adrift in the Equatorial Pacific*. I read this several years ago as part of a "reading around the world" challenge so I could check the Republic of Kiribati off my list.

Before we wrap up, I have a few more mysteries to mention. After watching the *Three Pines Mysteries* series on Amazon, I had to go read the books that inspired them. *A Fatal Grace* is the first book in the Louise Penny's Inspector Gamache series. The French Canadian setting is fascinating.

If you're a fan of my Mollie McGhie cozy mystery series, did you notice the little Easter egg about the prequel to that series, *Robbery at the Roller Derby*? One of the things I love about writing multiple series is including fun references like that and having crossover characters.

Finally, this list wouldn't be complete without a mention of a Three Investigators book—*The Secret of the Crooked Cat*.

I'd love to hear about what books you enjoy and if you've read any of the books I mentioned above. Shoot me an email at: ellenjacobsonauthor@gmail.com.

GRANDMA OLSON'S RECIPES

Ricotta Chocolate Chip Muffins

Everyone in the Olson family has a sweet tooth and these muffins are a big hit with them. The ricotta cheese keeps the muffins moist. They're a delicious after dinner treat or perfect with a cup of coffee in the morning. You might want to double the recipe because they're sure to get eaten up in no time!

Ingredients:

2 cups all purpose flour
2 teaspoons baking soda
1/2 teaspoon salt
1 cup full fat ricotta cheese
1/2 cup butter softened
3/4 cup granulated sugar
1 egg
1/4 cup milk
1 teaspoons vanilla
3/4 cup chocolate chips (regular or mini)

Directions:

1 – Place liners in a muffin pan or spray it with non-stick cooking spray. (Note: Recipe makes 12 muffins.)
2 – Pre-heat the oven to 350 degrees.
3 – Stir the flour, baking soda, and salt together in a bowl.

4 – Using an electric mixer, combine the ricotta cheese, sugar, and butter together in a separate bowl. Beat for 2-3 minutes until light and fluffy.

5 – Add the egg and milk to the ricotta mixture, mixing until smooth.

6 – Add the dry ingredients to the wet ingredients until just combined. Do not overmix.

7 – Stir in the chocolate chips.

8 – Scoop the batter into the muffin pan, dividing equally.

9 – Bake for 20-24 minutes until a toothpick comes out clean.

10 – Let the muffin pan cool on a wire rack for 10 minutes. Then remove the muffins from pan and let cool completely.

Coronation Chicken Salad

Grandma Olson decided to try a different twist on chicken salad by adding curry powder and mango chutney. Despite the fact that this recipe was originally created in honor of Queen Elizabeth's coronation, Grandpa Olson was not a fan. He's the kind of fellow who likes familiar food. Everyone else thought it was delicious.

Ingredients:

3 cups cooked chicken (a rotisserie chicken is a great time-saving option)

3/4 cup mayonnaise
2 tablespoons mango chutney (dice any larger pieces of mango into smaller pieces)
2 teaspoons curry powder
1 teaspoon lemon juice
Pinch of salt and ground pepper
1/2 cup slivered almonds
1/3 cup raisins (optional)

Directions:

1 – Dice the chicken and place into a large bowl.
2 – In a small bowl, mix the mayonnaise, chutney, curry powder, lemon juice, salt and pepper. Taste and add more curry powder if desired. (Note: Curry powders vary in how spicy they are.)
3 – Combine the mayonnaise mixture with the chicken.
4 – Stir in the almonds and and raisins into the chicken mixture.
5 – Refrigerate the chicken salad for at least an hour.
6 – Serve the chicken salad as a sandwich filling or over a bed of lettuce.

AUTHOR'S NOTE

Thank you so much for reading my book! If you enjoyed it, I'd be grateful if you would consider leaving a short review on the site where you purchased it and/or on Goodreads. Reviews help other readers find my books while also encouraging me to keep writing.

I had so much fun writing this book and drawing on my own experiences volunteering at my local library. Of course, it goes without saying that my volunteer duties do not include investigating murders. Thea Olson, on the other hand, isn't as lucky.

Many thanks to Cate, Duwan, Greg, Lisa, Melissa, and Mike for reading earlier drafts of this book and helping make it better. My husband is a proud born-and-bred North Dakotan and the inspiration for this series. I'm eternally grateful to him for his character and story ideas, not to mention his unfailing support of my writing career. Finally, I'm so appreciative of my amazing editor, Alecia Goodman, for her thoughtful edits and suggestions.

Find out more about me and my other books at ellenjacobsonauthor.com.

ABOUT THE AUTHOR

Ellen Jacobson is a chocolate obsessed cat lover who writes cozy mysteries and romantic comedies. After working in Scotland and New Zealand for several years, she returned to the States, lived aboard a sailboat, traveled around in a tiny camper, and is now settled in a small town in northern Oregon with her husband and an imaginary cat named Simon.

Find out more at ellenjacobsonauthor.com

ALSO BY ELLEN JACOBSON

North Dakota Library Mysteries

Planning for Murder
Murder at the Library
Poisoned by the Book

Mollie McGhie Mysteries

Robbery at the Roller Derby
Murder at the Marina
Bodies in the Boatyard
Poisoned by the Picr
Buried by the Beach
Dead in the Dinghy
Shooting by the Sea
Overboard on the Ocean
Murder Aboard the Mistletoe

The Mollie McGhie Cozy Mystery Collection: Books 1-3
The Mollie McGhie Cozy Mystery Collection: Books 4-6

Smitten with Travel Romantic Comedies

Smitten with Ravioli
Smitten with Croissants
Smitten with Strudel
Smitten with Candy Canes
Smitten with Baklava
Smitten with Caviar

The Smitten with Travel Collection: Books 1-3

Printed in Great Britain
by Amazon

50045818R00171